T0144779

The Son of
Clemenceau

The Son of Clemenceau

A Novel of Modern Love and Life

Alexandre Dumas, fils

MINT EDITIONS

The Son of Clemenceau: A Novel of Modern Love and Life was first published in the mid-1800s.

This edition published by Mint Editions 2021.

ISBN 9781513205328 | E-ISBN 9781513278728

Published by Mint Editions®

MINT
EDITIONS

minteditionbooks.com

Publishing Director: Jennifer Newens
Design & Production: Rachel Lopez Metzger
Project Manager: Micaela Clark
Typesetting: Westchester Publishing Services

Contents

I

STUDENT AND SOLDIER

The sunset-gun had been fired from the ramparts of the fortifications of Munich and the shadows were thickly descending on the famous old city of Southern Germany. The evening breeze in this truly March weather came chill over the plain of stones where Isar flowed darkly, and at the first puff of it, forcing him to wind his cloak round him, a lonely wanderer in the low quarter recognized why "the City of Monks" was also called "the Realm of Rheumatism."

The new town, which he had not yet seen, might justify yet another of its nicknames, "the German Athens," but here were, in this southern and unfashionable suburb, only a few modern structures, and most of the quaint and rather picturesque dwellings, overhanging the stores, dated anterior to the filling up of the town moat in 1791.

The stranger was clearly fond of antiquarian spectacles, for his eye, though too youthful to belong to a Dryasdust professor, and unshaded by the almost universal colored spectacles of the learned classes, gloated on the mansions, once inhabited by the wealthy burghers. They were irregular in plan and period of erection; the windows had ornamental frames of great depth, but some were blocked up, which gave the facades a sinister aspect; the walls had not only ornamental tablets in stucco, but, in a better light, would have shown rude fresco paintings not unworthy mediæval Italian dwellings. Many of the fronts resembled the high poops of the castellated ships of three hundred years ago, and they cast a shadow on the muddy pavement. As they resembled ships, the slimy footway seemed the strand where they had been beached by the running out of the tide.

As the darkness increased, the amateur of architecture became more solitary in the streets where the peasants in long black coats, their holiday wear, were hurrying to leave by the gates, and the storekeepers had renounced any hope of taking more money, in this ward, gloomy, neglected and remote from the mode, no display of goods was made after dark. But the man, finding novel effects in the obscurity, continued to gaze on the rickety houses and bestowed only a transient portion of his curiosity on the few wayfarers who stolidly trudged past him to cross a bridge of no importance a little beyond his post.

One or two of the passengers, rather those of the gentler sex than the rude one, had, however, given attention to the figure which the flowing cloak did not wholly muffle. With his dark complexion and slender form, not much in keeping with the thickset and heavy-footed natives, and his glistening black eyes, he made the corner where he ensconced himself appear the nook where an Italian or Spanish gallant was waylaying a rival in love.

Presently there was a change in the lighting of the scene, the gloom had become trying to his sight. Not only were two lamps lit on the small bridge, one at each end in the ornate iron scroll work, which Quintin Matsys would not have disavowed, but, overhead, the sky was reddened by the reflection of the thousands of gas jets in the north and west; the gay and spendthrift city was awakening to life and mirth while the working town was going to bed. This glimmer gave a fresh attraction to the architectural features, and still longer detained the spectator.

"Superb!" he muttered, in excellent German, without local peculiarity, as if he had learned it from professors, but there was a slight trace of an accent not native. "It has even now the effect which Gustavus Adolphus termed: 'a gilded saddle on a lean jade!'" Then, shivering again, he added, struck as well by the now completely deserted state of the ways as by the cold wind: "How bleak and desolate! One could implore these carved wooden statues to come down and people the odd, interesting streets!"

He was about to leave the spot, when, as though his wish was gratified, a strange sound was audible in the narrow and devious passages, between tottering houses, and those even more squalid in the rear, a commingling of shuffling and stamping feet, the smiting of heavy sticks on uneven stones and the dragging of wet rags.

Struck with surprise, if not with apprehension, he shrank back into the over-jutting porch of an old residence, with sculptured armorial bearings of some family long ago abased in its pride. Here he peered, not without anxiety.

By the exact programme carried out in cities by the divisions of its population, a new contingent were coming from their resting-places to substitute themselves for the honest toilers on the thoroughfares; each cellar and attic in the rookeries were exuding the horrible vermin which shun the wholesome light of day.

The spruce trees, stuck in tubs of sand at a beer-house beyond the bridge, shuddered as though in disgust at this horde of Hans hastening to invade the district of hotels, supper-houses and gaming clubs, to beg or steal the means to survive yet another day.

For ten or fifteen minutes the stranger watched the beggars stream individually out of the mazes and, to his horror, form like soldiers for a review, along the street before him, up to the end of the bridge at one extremity and far along at the other end of the line. Some certainly spied him, for these wretches could see as lucidly as the felines in the night—their day from society having reversed their conditions. But, though these whispered the warning to one another, and he was the object of scrutiny, no one left his place, and soon as their backs were turned to him, he had no immediate uneasiness as regarded an attack, or even a challenge upon his business there.

Probably the good citizens were not ignorant that this meeting of the vagrants took place each evening, for not only were all store-doors closed hermetically, but the upper windows no longer emitted a scintillation of lamplight. The spy by accident concluded that he would raise his voice for help all in vain as far as the tradesmen were concerned. But he was brave, and he let increasing curiosity enchain him continuously.

From time out of mind the sage in velvet has serenely contemplated Diogenes in his tub; not that our philosopher seemed the treasurer of an Alexander!

Ranged at length in a long row, cripples, the blind, the young, the aged, it was a company of mendicants which eccentric painters would have given five years of life to have seen. Except for consumptive coughs, the misstep of a wooden leg of which the clumsy ferule slipped on a cobblestone, and the querulous whimper of a child, half-starved and imperfectly swaddled in a tattered shawl, on a flaccid bosom, the mob were silent in an expectation as intense as the lookers-on. The wind brought the whistle of the railway locomotives and the clanking of a steam-dredger in the river, like a giant toiling in massive chains.

For this platoon of vice and misery, crime and disorder, laziness and rapine, the stranger confidently expected to see a commander appear whose flashing, fearless eye, and upright, powerful frame, would account for the awe in which all were held.

What was his amazement, therefore, to perceive—while a tremor of emotion thrilled the line and announced the commander whom all awaited—a bent-up, scarcely human-shaped form, hardly to be acknowledged a woman's. It was enveloped in a heavily furred pelisse fitted for a man.

This singular object appeared up the trap of a cellarway, much like the opening of a sewer, on the opposite side of the street. She proceeded to review the vagabonds and put questions and issue orders to each, which were received like mandates from Cæsar by his legions. The voice was fine and shrill, the movements betokened vigor, but the whole impression was that the female captain-general of the beggars of Munich was far from young.

In the obscurity, and keeping in the background as he did, it was not possible for the stranger to scan her features; besides, they were veiled by the long hair of a Polish hunter's cap, with earflaps and a drooping foxtail, worn as the pompon but half-loosened in time. The eyes that inspected the file of vagrants, shone with undiminished force, and when they fell on the burliest and most impudent, these became quiet and submissive. In a word, the cohort of beggary yielded utter subserviency to this remarkable leader.

Questions and answers were uttered in a thieve's jargon which were sealed letters to the eavesdropper, but it seemed to him that they all addressed her as *Baboushka*! This struck him as more odd from its being a Slavonic title, meaning "grandmother." Was it possible that he had before him one of those prolific centenarians, truly a mother of the tribe, a gypsy queen to whom allegiance went undisputed and who rules the subterranean strata of society with fewer revolts against them than their sister rulers know, who sit on thrones in the fierce white light?

In any case, he was given no leisure for deciding the question, for an active urchin had whispered a word of caution which led the feminine general to direct a piercing glance toward him, and hasten to conclude her arrangements. The line broke up into little groups, though most of the men went singly, and all tramped over the little foot-bridge, which swung under the unusual mass.

Left alone, the vagrants' queen, placing her yellow and skinny hand on a weapon, perhaps, among her rags, resolutely moved toward the spy. He expected to be interrogated, for an attack was unlikely from a lone old woman; but he grasped his cane firmly.

Luckily, a noise of steps at the other end of the street checked the hag; she thrust back out of sight what had momentarily gleamed like the steel of a knife or brass of a pistol-barrel; listened again and stared;

ALEXANDRE DUMAS, FILS

then, muttering what was probably no prayer for the stranger's welfare, she crossed the street with amazing rapidity. The student, hearing a heavy military tread at the mouth of the street, expected to see her vanish down her burrow, but, to his astonishment, she proceeded toward the new-comer.

"The Schutzmaun," muttered he, as there loomed into sight a decidedly soldier-like man in a long cloak, thrown back to show the scarlet lining, and dragging a clanking sabre.

Relying on her good angel, apparently, the witch boldly passed him, and it seemed to the watcher that a sign of understanding was rapidly exchanged between them. Baboushka seemed to enjoin caution for the stranger hooked up his trailing sabre, wrapped his cloak around him and came on less noisily. Certainly the old hag did not beg of him, but hastened to leave the street.

If the new-comer had been the night guardian coming on duty, the student might have lost any misgiving about the vagrants or their ruler; but he was not sure that in him was a friend.

This was an officer, not a gendarme or military policeman. Cloak and uniform were dark blue and fine. He bore himself with the swagger of a personage of no inconsiderable rank, and also of some degree in the nobility. Tall, burly, overbearing, the stranger took a dislike to him from this one glance, and would have hesitated to appeal to him for assistance had he felt in danger.

But the beggars had flocked into the rich quarter, and their chieftainess vanished. He allowed the military gentleman to pass, and was not sorry to see him cross the bridge with a steady, haughty step, which made his heel ring on each plank. But, on reaching the farther end, to the surprise of the watcher, his carriage immediately altered; his step became cautious and, like the other whom he had not noticed, he skulked in a doorway. He might have been thought a visitor there, but, at the next moment, his red whiskers reappeared between the turned-up collar of his mantle as he showed his head under the cornice of oak.

For what motive had the officer and nobleman stooped to skulking and prying. One alone would amply exonerate the son of Mars— devotion to Venus. And the architectural student, not fearing to pass the soldier in his excusable ambush for a sweetheart, since his route over the bridge into the new city, and not wishful to spoil the lover's sport, since he was of the age to sympathize, prepared to leave his nook.

But it was fated that continual impediments were to be thrown in his path on this eventful night. He had hardly taken two steps out of his covert, which kept him hidden from the officer but revealed him to any one approaching in the street, before a third individual of singular mien caught his view and transfixed him with a thrill so sharp, poignant and profound that a stroke of lightning would not have more dreadfully affected him.

And yet, it was a woman—young by her step, light and quick as the antelope's, graceful by her movements, charming by her outlines which a poor, thin woolen wrapper imperfectly shrouded. She enchanted by the mere contour; it was her weird burden which appalled the watcher. In one hand, suspended horizontally, lengthwise parallel to her course, she held what seemed by shape and somber hue to be an infant's coffin.

Her dark and brilliant eyes had descried him from the distance, but, in an instant recognizing that he was neither one of the usual nocturnal denizens nor another sort of whom she need entertain dread, she came on apace.

Indeed, he was far from resembling the vagrants. He was clad without any attention to the toilette, after the manner of the German student, who likes to affront the Pharisee but without overmuch eccentricity. Under the voluminous cloak, warranted by the chilly wind, a tight-fitting tunic of dark green cloth, caught in by a broad buff leather belt with the clasp of a University, admirably defined the shapeliness of a slight but manly form. His hair, black as the raven's wing, was worn long and came curling down on his shoulders; his complexion was dark but clear. But the whole appearance was of a marvel in physical excellencies; a physiologist would have pointed to him as a model and result of the combination of all desirable traits in both his progenitors. His attitude, checked in the advance, denoted this perfection. The young woman, set at ease by her glances and that peace which true symmetry inspires, continued her way, averting her head with calculation, but he felt sure that she was not offended.

He could laugh at the mistake he had made for, at this close encounter, he perceived that what in the tragic mood originated by the review of beggars in the shades of night, he had taken to be a child's casket, was a violin-case. The girl—she was perhaps but sixteen—had the artist's eye, black, fiery, deep and winning, while haughty for the vulgar worshiper; her hair was treated in a fantastic fashion as unlike that of the staid German maiden as its hue of black was the opposite of the traditional flaxen. Even in the feeble street-lamplight, she appeared, with her finely chiseled features of an Oriental type, handsome enough to melt an anchorite, and in the beholder a flood of passion gushed up and expanded his heart—devoid of such a mastering emotion before. He believed this was love! Perhaps it was love—real, true, indubitable love—but there is a mock-love with so much to advance in its favor that it has won many a battle where the genuine feeling has fought long in vain.

Sharing some shock not unlike his own in extent and sharpness, the girl with the violin-case had paused just perceptibly in an unconscious attitude which kept in the lamplight her bust, tightly encased in a faded but elegant Genoa brocade jacket, with copper lace ornamentation, coming down upon a promising curve, clothed in a similarly theatrical skirt of flowered satin and China silk braid. On her wrists were bracelets and on her ungloved hands many rings, with stones rather too large to be taken for genuine on a woman promenading alone at such an hour. Conjoined with the musical instrument, the attire confirmed the student in his first impression after the tragic one, that this was a performer in one of the numerous dance-houses of the popular region, bordering the fashionable one.

He almost regretted this conclusion, for the girl's forehead was so high, her eyes so lofty and her delicate mouth so impressed with a proud and energetical curl that no ambition would seem beyond the flight of one thus beautiful and high-spirited.

Whatever the revolution she had exercised over him, he dared not avow it, such respect did she inspire, and on her recovering from her fleeting emotion, he let her resume her way without a word to detain her.

She had not reached the first plank of the bridge before he suddenly remembered the officer, like himself, in ambush; and in the same manner as love—if that were love—had clutched his heart with the swiftness of an eagle seizing its quarry, another sentiment, as fierce and overpowering, jealousy, stung him to the quick.

As he glanced—but he had not taken his eyes off her, not even to look if the military officer were still at his post—she had swept her worsted wrapper round to set her foot on the first board of the bridge; and he caught a glimpse, delightful and bewildering, of a foot, long but slim and delicately modeled, and of a faultless ankle, in a vermilion silk stocking and low-cut cordovan leather slipper—as theatrical as the rest of her attire. Something innately aesthetical in the student, which made him adore the exquisitely wrought, impelled him now to be the slave—the devotee—the worshiper of this masterpiece of Nature.

Perhaps she stood in need of a defender?

II

Soldier's Sword and Wander-Staff

The place was historically favored for adventures. In 1543, the riot of Knights and Knaves had begun here. On the bridge which preceded this structure, a band of young noblemen had taken possession of the passage more important then, as this now foul and noisome channel, into which the effluvia of the breweries and tanneries was discharged, was a strong and pellucid tributary of the Isar. They levied tribute on the burghers, kissing the comely women and not scrupling to cut the purses of the master-tradesmen; in this, imitating the mode of operation of their country cousins, the robber barons in the mountains to the south, or over the river in the opposite direction.

But, as for the third or fourth time, the student was on the verge of quitting his haven, another interrupter arose. Pausing at the head of the bridge, prompted by natural caution or instinct, for the officer remained prudently invisible to her, the girl, with the violin-case, looked over her shoulder and beckoned to some one on the further side of the astonished student.

The desert was becoming animated, indeed, as he had wished, for, in the hazy opening, a man appeared, carrying under one arm what seemed a musket or blunderbuss, while leaning the other hand on a staff which might be the one to rest the firearm on. He had a flat felt hat on, with wide shaggy margins, ornamented with a yellow cord in contrast with its inky dye, and a dingy, often mended old cavalry-soldier's russet cloak, covering him from a long, full grey beard to the feet, encased in patched shoes. The aspect of a Jew peddler in the pictures of the Dutch school, who had armed himself to defend his pack of thread and needles on the highway.

But, as before, nearness dispelled the romantic conceit: the supposed gun resolved itself into a Turko-phone, or Oriental flute, while, on the other hand, the bright eye and well-shaped features, with the venerable impression suggested by the beard, lifted the wearer into a high place for reverence. Just as the girl was unrivaled for beauty, this man, a near relative, perhaps her father, would have few equals in the councils of his tribe.

While not old, spite of the grey in his beard, illness had enfeebled him, for he needed the walking-staff. The brisk pace of his daughter had left him far behind and it cost him an effort to make up for the delay. But in parental love he found the force, and quite nimbly he passed the student without observing him in his haste to join his daughter.

At the sight of him coming, she had not waited for his arm, but retaken her course. She was half way over the bridge when he began to ascend the gentle slope, and when he was arduously following with the summit well before him, the officer emerged abruptly from his covert. He must have been calculating on this moment and this separation to which Baboushka had no doubt contributed. She now loomed into view. Repulsed by the Jew in his detestation of beggars—for while the Christian accepts poverty as a misfortune to which resignation is one remedy, he regards it as an affliction to be violently removed—she hesitated to continue her annoyance. The bridge was so narrow that he had no difficulty, thanks to the length of his arms, in placing a hand on each rail, so that, as he bent his broad, smiling face forward between them, he effectively barred the way. With a tone which he intended to be winning and tender, but which nature had not allowed him to modulate very sweetly, he said:

"Divine songstress of Freyer Brothers' Brewery Harmonista Cellars!" She stopped quickly and faced half round, so as to be in a better position for retreat if he made an advance toward her. "In the hall on Thursday—when you made the circuit with the cup for the collection after your delightful ballad—you refused me even a reply to my request for an interview. That was for the favor of a salute from those somewhat thin but honeyed lips! Now, there is nobody by and I mean to be rewarded for the bouquets I have nightly sent you!"

"Father!" cried the Jewess, too frightened by the position of her assailant to flee.

"Your father? Bah!" with a contemptuous glance at the old man approaching only too slowly. "I repeat, there is no one by! *That* I arranged for."

The speaker had red curly hair like his whiskers; his brow was not narrow but his eyebrows overhung; his face was flushed with animation and carnal desire—perhaps by potations, though his large lower jaw denoted ample animal courage. He was powerful enough in the long arms and strong hands to have mastered the girl and her father, but it was not the dread of his prowess physically which awed the daughter of the race still proscribed in this part of Germany.

ALEXANDRE DUMAS, FILS

Frederick von Sendlingen, Baron of ancient creation, enjoyed a wide fame among the knot of noble carousers who strove to make one corner of Munich a pale reflection of the "fast" end of Paris and Vienna. A major in a crack heavy cavalry regiment, allowed for family reasons to remain in the garrison after it had been removed elsewhere, he enjoyed enviable esteem from his superiors and the hatred and dislike of all others. Though inclined to court after the manner of the pillager who has captured a city, his boisterous addresses pleased the wanton matrons and, more naturally, the facile Cythereans of the music halls and dance-houses.

At an early hour, he had cast his handkerchief, like an irresistible sultan, at the chief attraction of the beer cellar, which he named—the so-called "La Belle Stamboulane," and baffled in all his less brutal modes of attack, he had recourse to one which better suited his custom.

It looked as though he had lost time in not putting it into operation before, since the girl, around whom, taking one stride, he threw his arms, could not, by her feeble resistance, prevent him snatching a kiss. As for her father, casting down his turkophone, and raising his staff in both hands, his valorous approach went for little, as his blow would have been as likely to fall upon his daughter as the ruffian.

While he was bewildered and his stick was raised in air, the latter, perceiving his danger, did not scruple to show his contempt for one of the despised race whom he likewise scorned for his weakness, by dealing him a kick in the leg with his heavy boot which, fairly delivered, would have broken an oaken post. Though avoiding its full force, the unhappy father was so painfully struck that he staggered back to the opposite rail of the bridge and, clapping both hands to the bruise on the shin, groaned while he strove in vain to overcome the paralyzing agony. From that moment he was compelled to remain as a stranger in action to the outrage.

Still struggling, though with little hope, the girl saw the defeat of her natural champion with sympathetic anguish. Though he had not spied the student, she had regarded him with no faint opinion of his manliness for—repelling the kind of proud self-reliance of her race to have no recourse to strangers during persecution—she lifted her voice with a confidence which startled her rude adorer.

"Help! help from this ruffian-gentleman!"

"Silence, you fool," rejoined Sendlingen. "I tell you, the coast is clear—for I have arranged all that. It is simple strategy to secure one's flanks—"

"Help!" repeated the songstress, redoubling her efforts—not to escape, which was out of the question, but to shield her mouth from contact with the red moustaches, hovering over it like the wings of a bloodstained bird of rapine.

As this repetition of the appeal, steps clattered on the bridge, and the officer lifted his head. He may have expected Baboushka or one of her fraternity, and the tall, slender student, who had flung off his cloak to run more swiftly, gave him a surprise. The agile and intelligent girl took the opportunity with commendable speed, and glided out of the major's relaxing grasp like a wasp from under the spider's claws. She retreated as far as where her father tried to stand erect, and helping him up, led him prudently down the bridge slope so that they might continue their flight. It would have been the basest ingratitude to depart without seeing the result of the interference, and the two lingered, though it would have been wiser to let the two Christians bite and tear each other without witnesses of another creed, and with the witness of none.

It was a free spectacle, but, if it had cost their week's salary at the casino, it would have been worth the money.

As the major had empty hands after the loss of his prize, the student had the quixotic delicacy to make the offer in dumbshow to lay aside his cane and undertake to chastise the insulter of womanhood with the naked fist. But this is a weapon almost unknown in the sword-bearing class which Von Sendlingen adorned, and, infuriated by the civilian intervening at the culmination of his daring plan, to say nothing of the annoying thought that his failure would be no secret from the old hag, his accomplice, looking on at the extremity of the bridge, he yielded to the worst devil in his heart. He inclined to the most high-handed and hectoring measure. Whipping out his sabre with a rapid gesture, and merely muttering a discourteous and grudging: "Be on your guard!" he dealt a cut at the student which threatened to cleave him in two.

The other was on the alert; he had suspected one capable of such an outrage, likewise capable of worse, and he parried the coward's blow so dexterously with his cane that it was the soldier who was thrown off his balance. A second blow, with the tremendous sweep of the stick held at arm's length, tested the metal of the blade to its utmost, and, as the wielder's hand was thoroughly palsied, drove it out of the opening fingers, and all heard it splash in the black and pestiferous waters under the bridge.

Von Sendlingen would almost have preferred the blow falling on his head. An officer, whose reputation in fencing was no mean one, to be disarmed by a student who swung but his road-cane! This was not all: he had lost his sabre, and, noble though he was, he had to pass the vigorous inspection of his weapons like the humblest private soldier! The absence of the regimental sword might cause degradation, ruin militarily and socially! And all for a "music-hall squaller"—and a Jewess at that!

He ground his teeth, and his eyes were filled with angry fire. His face bore a greater resemblance to a tiger's than a man's, and had not the victor in this first bout possessed a stout heart, he might have regretted that he had commenced so well, so terrible would be the retaliation.

All the animal in the man being roused, he longed to throw himself on his antagonist to grasp his throat, but the successful use of the cudgel against the sword indicated that this was an adept at quarter-staff and a man with naked hands would have easily been beaten if pitted with him. Sendlingen, warily and rapidly surveying the limited field of combat, caught sight of the Jew's walking-staff and sprang for it with an outcry of savage glee and hope.

On perceiving this move, in spite of the pain still crippling him, the old man started to retrace his steps to regain possession of his weapon, but he was soon distanced by the younger one.

Armed with this staff, the officer, remembering his student days, when he, too, was an expert swinger of the cane, a Bavarian mountaineer's weapon with which duels to the death are not unseldom fought, he stood before the student.

"Had you been a gentleman," began the major, with a sullen courtesy, extorted from him by the gallantry of his antagonist.

"A stick to a dog!" retorted the latter, falling into the position of guard with an ease and accuracy which caused the other to begin his work by feints and attacks not followed up too rashly, in order to test him.

This time, it was the stouter and more brutal man who played cautiously and the younger and more refined who was spurred into recklessness by the contiguity of the fair Helen—or, rather, Esther—who had caused the fray.

The girl stood at the end of the bridge, opposite to Baboushka at hers, there making them simple lookers-on. The old Jew seemed eager to join in the struggle, but the staves were in continual swing, and he could not draw near without the risk of having a shoulder dislocated, or, at least, his knuckles severely rapped. In the gloom, his hovering about the involved pair would have led an opera-goer to have seen in him the demon who thus actively presides at the fatal duel of Faust and Valentine.

But the conflict, whatever the major's wariness, could not be long protracted, for canes of this sort are tiring to the arm, unlike smallswords; he was still on the defensive when the student assailed him with a shower of blows which taxed all his skill and nerve, and the strength of the staff which he had borrowed from his foe. Well may one suspect "the gifts of an enemy!" as the student might have cited: "*Timeo danaos*," etc. At the very moment when the officer's head was most in peril, while he guarded it with the staff held horizontally in both hands separated widely for the critical juncture, it ominously cracked at the reception of a vigorous blow—it parted as though a steel blade had severed it, and the unresisted cane came down on his skull with crushing force.

Out of the two cavities which the broken staff now presented, rattled several gold coins. At the sight, the old hag scrambled toward where the major had fallen senseless. The Jew, after picking up the broken pieces of wood, would have lingered to recover those of the precious metal though at cost of a scuffle with Baboushka. But his daughter rebuked him in their language with an indignant tone, which brought him to his senses in an instant. She seized him by the arm, and hurried him away at last.

After a brief survey of the defeated man, wavering between the fear that he had killed him and the prompting to see to his hurts, if the case were not fatal, the student took to flight in the direction the beautiful girl had chosen. He well knew that this was a grave matter, and that he trod on burning ground. At twenty paces farther, he remembered his cloak, but on the bridge were now clustered several shadows vying with Baboushka in picking up the coin before raising the unfortunate Von Sendlingen.

Not a light had appeared at the windows of the houses, not a window had opened for a night-capped head to be thrust forth, not a voice had echoed the Jewess's call for the watch. It was not to be doubted that Footbridge street had allowed more murderous outrages to occur without anyone running the risk of catching a cold or a slash of a sabre.

"A cut-throat quarter, that is it," remarked the student, still too excited to feel the cold and want of his outer garment. "After all, one cannot travel from Berlin to Paris without getting some soot on the cheek and a cinder or two in the eye. In the same way it is not possible to see life and go through this world without being smeared with a little blood or smut."

While talking to himself, he smoothed his dress and curled his dark and fine moustache, projecting horizontally and not drooping. He had walked so fast that he had overtaken the Jews, delayed as the girl was by her father's lameness, and having to carry the violin in its case which she had recovered and preciously guarded.

"What an audacious bully that was," the student continued; "but even a good cat loses a mouse now and then."

The pair seemed to expect him to join them, but as he was about to do so, at the mouth of a narrow and unlighted alley, he heard the measured tramp of feet indicating the patrol.

Already the character of the streets and houses changed: there were vistas of those large buildings which give one the impression that Munich is planned on too generous a scale for its population. Only here and there was a roof or front suggestive of the Middle Ages, and they may have been in imitation; the others were stately and were classical, and the avenues became spacious.

All at once, while the student was watching the semi-military constables approach, he heard an uproar toward the bridge. The major had been discovered by quite another sort of folk than the allies of Baboushka, and the alarm was given.

To advance was to invite an arrest which would result in no pleasant investigation.

He had tarried too long as it was. The watchman's horn—tute-horn—sounded at the bridge and the squad responded through their commander; whistles also shrilled, being police signals. The student was perceived. It was a critical moment. The next moment he would be challenged, and at the next, have a carbine or sabre levelled at his breast. He retired up the alley, precipitately, wondering where the persons whom he befriended had disappeared so quickly.

A very faint light gleamed from deeply within, at the end of a crooked passage through a lantern-like projection at a corner. A number of iron hooks bristled over his head as if for carcasses at a butcher's, although their innocent use was to hang beds on them to air. On a tarnished plate he deciphered "ARTISTES' ENTRANCE," and while perplexed, even as the gendarmes appeared at the mouth of this blind-alley, a long and taper hand was laid on his arm and a voice, very, very sweet, though in a mere murmur, said irresistibly:

"Come! come in, or you will be lost!" He yielded, and was drawn into a corridor under the oriel window, where the air was pungent with the reek of beer, tobacco-smoke, orange-peel, cheese and caraway seeds.

III

"The Jingle-Jangle"

The person to whom the shapely hand and musical voice belonged, conducted the student along the narrow passage to a turning where she halted, under a lamp with a reflector which threw them in that position into the shade. The passage was divided by the first lobby, and on the lamp was painted, back to back: "Men," "Ladies;" besides, a babble of feminine voices on the latter side betrayed, as the intruder suspected from the previous placard, that he had entered a place of entertainment by the stage-door, a Tingel-Tangel, or Jingle-Jangle, as we should say.

It was the Jewess who was the Ariadne to this maze. Seen in the light, at close range, with the enchanting smile which a woman always finds for the man who has won her gratitude by supplementing her deficiency in strength and courage with his own, she was worthier love than ever. At this view, too, he was sure that, unlike too many of the *divas* of these *spielungs*, or dens, she was not one of the stray creatures who sell pleasure to some and give it to others, and for themselves keep only shame—fatal ignominy, wealth at best very unsubstantial, and if, at last, winners, they laugh—one would rather see them weeping.

"What's your name?" she inquired, quickly. "I am Rebecca Daniels, whom they call on the Bills 'La Belle Stamboulane'—though I have never been farther east than Prague," she added with a contemptuous smile. "That was my father, whose maltreatment you so promptly but I fear so severely chastised. But your name?" impatiently.

"I am a student of Wilna University, traveling according to custom of the college, through Germany and to make the Italian Art Tour. I am Claudius Ruprecht."

"Not noble?" she inquired, sadly, on hearing two Christian names and none of family, for her people treasure the pride of ancestry.

"I am an orphan. I never knew my family. Perhaps, as I am of age, I shall soon be informed. But—"

"Enough! time is getting on, and we cannot long stay in privacy here—the passage-way for the performers. This is Freyers' Hall, where I sing—where I was a player. But my father can speak to you in the public room and see to your safety—for I fear this night's affair will end ill. But do not you fear! neither my father nor I have the powerlessness which that noble ruffian seemed to think is ours. You, at least, shall be saved—even though you killed that brute."

"I do not think that, unless his head is not so hard as his heart."

She opened a narrow door in the dirty wall. It was brighter in the capacious place thus shown.

"Go in and sit down anywhere. My father will be with you in a few minutes. We were so delayed that they feared we would not arrive for 'our turn.' They were glad of the excuse—I fancy they were told it might occur—and they are trying to break our agreement. But never mind! that is but a bread-and-butter business for us. For you, it will be life and death, if that officer be slain."

Claudius, the student, mechanically obeyed the gentle impulsion her hand imparted to him on the shoulder, and walked through the side-door. A number of benches were before him with corresponding narrow tables, and he sat down at one, and looked round.

He found himself in a very long, rectangular hall, low in the ceiling in proportion to the length, once brightly decorated, but faded, smoked and tarnished. On the walls, in panels, between tinted pilasters of a pseudo-Grecian design, were views of the principal towns of Germany and Austria, the details obliterated in the upper part by smoke and in the lower by greasy heads and hands. Around the sides, a dais held benches and tables similar to those on the floor. At the far end was a bar for beer and other liquors less popular, and an entrance from a main street, screened and indirect, down steps at another level than the rear or stage door. Where Claudius sat was a small stage with footlights and curtain complete, and an orchestra for a miniature piano such as are used in yachts, and six musicians; the performers sat to face the audience respectfully in the good Old German style.

The lighting was by means of clusters of gas-jets at intervals in the long ceiling and along the walls. The announcement of the items of attraction appearing on the stage was made by changeable sliding cards in framework at the sides of the stage; to the left the name of the *scena* was exhibited, that of the artist on the other.

When Claudius took his seat, the other places were almost all empty; but they soon began to fill up. The majority of the spectators seemed to be of the tradesman and workman class, with their wives and daughters, but the stranger, who had been so surreptitiously "passed in," was not blind to the presence of a more offensive element. There were faces as villainous as any under the immediate command of Grandmother "Baboushka;" and their dress was not much better. More than one dandy of the gutter nursed the head of a club called significantly the "lawbreaker's canes of crime," with a distant air of the fop sucking his clouded amber knob or silver shepherd's-crook. In more than one group were horse-copers, and their kin the market-gardeners' thieves and country wagoners' pests, who not only lighten the loads on the way to the city market on the road, but plunder the drivers after they receive their salesmoney by cheating at cards.

The student, crowded in by this mixed throng, began to doubt the providential quality of the intervention saving him from an explanation to the police; it was very like leaping from the proverbial frying-pan into the fire.

At this stage in his reflections, he felt that a person in the next seat had risen and he soon perceived that he had politely, or from a stronger reason, given up his place to another. This was the old Jew, but he would not have known him by his dress, it was so changed for the better; the fine profile, the venerable beard which an Arab Sheikh would have reverenced, and the sharp, intelligent eyes were unaltered.

"Do you speak Latin?" inquired Daniels in that tongue.

But Claudius, though reading the dead tongue fluently, pronounced it after the University manner, and felt that he could not sustain a dialogue with one who followed the Italian usage. He could speak Italian, however, for he had long studied it to be at home in the world of Art.

"The officer was not killed," remarked the Jew, and before his new acquaintance could express his relief, he added gravely, "but he has been spirited away."

"Then it's those vagabonds—"

"Of whom that old *Tausend-Kunstlerin* (witch of a thousand tricks) is in the position of parent? I guess as much. He said he had connived with her, one who is the actual though occult ruler of the filthy region. We have had to pay her blackmail regularly, like the other artists, for we are obliged to go home after midnight. Well, if he is in their hands, it is among congenial spirits. Tell me your name and as much of your affairs as you please to enlighten me with. I am bound to assist you as far as possible—though my debt to you will ever remain uncanceled. I am Daniel Daniels, of Odessa, Marseilles, and elsewhere, and an introduction to my correspondent nearest where you sojourn is not to be despised."

Impressed with his tone, the young man related his life-story succinctly.

He had a dreamy remembrance of a long journey, lastly in a sledge, buried in fur robes, his clearer later memories were of a happy home in Poland, in the country, where, though strangers, all were kind to the lonely orphan. There was a mystery about his parentage; his mother was probably a native as he acquired the language as easily as the art of eating, the peasants said. His father had been killed, he thought, on one of those riots which, in a small way, repeat the olden revolutions of Poland against the triumvirate of oppression, Austria, Prussia and Russia. But he had heard a tutor say, when he was not supposed in hearing, that he had perished by the executioner's steel.

"A death honorable as under the bullets," said Claudius, but half doubtingly.

As became a man who abhorred homicide in any shape, Daniels made no reply.

"At the age of eighteen, while at the University, I was given a private tutor in art and architecture, to which I had a bent. He was a Frenchman and I acquired his elegant tongue with that well-known facility of us Poles in attaining proficiency in the Western ones. Armed with that and Italian—"

"Which you speak with finish," interrupted the Jew.

"I expect my Italian and French tour to be delightful. But I am not over the frontier yet, and hardly will be soon if my passport is commented upon by an authority cognizant of this night's adventure."

"I regret to find that it was deliberately planned," resumed Daniels. "My daughter's virtue has raised more hostility under this roof than even her talent. The proprietor is a notorious rascal, but he is too useful to the profligate among the town officials to be reprimanded. The police, too, wink at his personal misdoings, because he is always their friend to deliver the criminals who make this haunt their rendezvous. All those painted women, as well as the waiter-girls, are spies and Dalilahs who betray the Samsons of crime to the police at any given moment. That would be neither here nor there, however, if my daughter and I were allowed to conclude our engagement—which, believe me, would never have been signed if we had guessed the character of the resort. Not only would they lodge me in prison for a pretended attempt to elude my contract, but they seek to throw my poor Rebecca into the arms of such reprobates as this Major the Baron. The hag whom you noticed is not unconcerned in the plot. It is a protégé of hers—a lovely young girl, guileless in appearance as a cherub, whom they would substitute for my girl, if she had been detained to-night. In fact—"

He paused. The orchestra had played and two or three vocalists had appeared and sang, without Claudius, absorbed in this conversation, noticing that the entertainment had commenced. A little fat man in a ruffled and embroidered shirt, buff waistcoat with crystal buttons, knee breeches and silk stockings of reproachless black, and steel buckled shoes, had come before the curtain, sticking one thumb in his waistband and the other in his vest armhole, to display a huge seal ring and a mammoth diamond hoop, respectively, as well as his idea of ease in company. He announced in a high flute-like voice that in consequence of indisposition, which a sworn medical affirmation confirmed—here he raised a laugh by sticking his tongue in his cheek— "La Belle Stamboulane" would not appear—might have to depart for Constantinople for convalescence, but that the bewitching Fraulein von Vieradlers—one of the few authentic *noble* vocalists on the variety stage—following in the footsteps of certain princesses—would oblige, for the first time on any stage, with selections from her repertoire, etc.

This was concerted, for the outburst of applause, started by the most sinister of aspect among the auditors, was vehement and so contagious that the *hussah* was unanimous as the stage-manager retired.

La Belle Stamboulane was already eclipsed! so evanescent is theatrical fame. Of all the audience, only one felt indignant, and that was the student Claudius, who had not heard her sing or wear stage costumes!

"All is over," observed Daniels placidly. "I cannot cope with these rogues. I must go and join my daughter and get our dresses to our lodgings; thankful if we succeed so far. In about an hour, will you not call, when we will resume our conversation which I wish to have, and with practical gain to you. This is the card of our hotel. It is not aristocratic, but once there, you will be safe."

He spoke with such tranquil assurance that Claudius had not a doubt. He took the card, read the address: "Hotel Persepolitan," so that if he lost the card, it might be in his mind, and nodded with a kind of gratefulness. The father of a beautiful woman is not like any other man in the world to a young man, who is not indifferent to her.

Following the old Jew with his gaze to the narrow side-door leading to behind-the-scenes, Claudius thought that, in the brief period of its opening and closing, he spied the bright black orbs of the Jewess striving to catch a glimpse even so transient of him. It did not need this encouragement to make him resolve to respond to the invitation.

An hour would soon pass, even in this tedious recreation. He felt also some resentment and curiosity to see the person whom the director of these Munich circeans considered in adequate succession to the peerless Stamboulane. The announcement had at least kindled the public: being plebeian, the promised aristocrat was already discussed. The family was existent, whether this variety vocalist was legitimately a daughter being another question. Vieradlers was a barony that had a right to fly its four eagles—as the name signifies—in the face of the double-headed king of the tribe. The baron was the latest of an old Bavarian line, famous in story. One of his ancestors was eagle-bearer to Cæsar after the defeat of Hermann. The continuators had always been near the emperors. There might be a drop of imperial blood in the child who had so strangely degenerated as to prefer royalty on the stage to that of the court and country-house.

"She may be good-looking," thought Claudius, "for I have noticed that where the men are uncomely the women are often the reverse. A Berlin professor has boldly likened the male Bavarian to the gorilla and the caricaturists have taken his cue. They are of the beer-barrel shape, coarse, rough, quarrelsome and quick to enter into a fight. It is the national dish of roast goose—a pugnacious bird—and bread of oatmeal that does it. They may well have one beauty of the sex among them. And the carnation on the cheeks of these waitresses is so remarkable that they find rouge superfluous. They are dull, and yet the twinkle in their eyes indicates cunning."

Before him, the next seat was occupied by two gentlemen. They spoke in French, thinking no one would comprehend their conversation. They were discussing the ascending star, about which one had a deeper knowledge than the subjects of Baboushka.

"She is the cause of the disgrace of the Grand-Chamberlain of a northern kingdom," said this well-informed man. "He has been obliged to send in his grand cross of the Royal Order and his rank in the Holy Empire, after what was almost a revolution in the palace. He is a man over sixty, who was in Russia on an important mission, when he met by chance this young girl, whose mother was married to a noble,

ALEXANDRE DUMAS, FILS

although the elder sister of one of those beauties notorious for their depravity in Paris. Perhaps, though, she secured her husband before her sister won this dubious celebrity. At all events, she lived blamelessly, but *bad* blood does not lie! This girl seems to aim at the reputation of her aunt, the celebrated Iza, whose portrait was painted, her figure copied in immortal marble, and her charms sung by French bards. At all events, she bewitched the old Count von Raackensee, who took her on a tour through our country and Austria. It was at Vienna that he, an old statesman and courtier, committed the folly of presenting her as his daughter! The truth came out—Austria and Prussia made remonstrances, and he was compelled to resign his office or this witch. He would not give her up and so he was punished."

"Punished?"

"Yes; he went on to live at Nice, where he had bought a villa in foresight for some such day of disgrace. The Circe was to follow him, but, instead of that, she has shaken off the golden links and condescends to stay a week in Munich to amuse us coarse swiggers of beer."

IV

The Star is Dead Long Live the Star!

B y listening to others and observing them, man obtains the material for self-preservation. Evidently this star of the minor stage was a woman to be avoided; a rising light which might scar the sight and burn the fingers of too venturesome an admirer. Claudius had a premonition that he ought to go out and kill the few minutes in strolling the streets, before keeping the appointment, even at the risk of being questioned by the police. But he overcame the impulsion, and waited to face what might be a danger the more.

All the hall, by instinct and from the stories circulating—perhaps circulated by the agents of the management—divined that no common attraction was to be presented. Besides, to displace La Belle Stamboulane worthily on the stage, that chosen arena where the female gladiator carries the day, a miracle of beauty, wit and skill was requisite. Elsewhere, ability, practice, art, artifice, many gifts and accomplishments may triumph, but the fifth element as indispensable as the others, air, water, fire and earth—it is *love*, which legitimately monopolizes the theatre for its exhibition and glorification. Men and women come to such places of amusement to hear love songs, see love scenes, and share in the fictitious joys and sorrows of love, which they long to enact in reality. Nothing is above love; nothing equals it. He reigns as a master in a temple, with woman as the high-priestess, and man the victim or the chosen reward.

Preceding the novelty, a bass-singer roared a drinking-song, in which he likened human life to a brewer's house, in which some quenched their thirst quickly and departed; others stayed to quaff, jest, tell stories to cronies, before staggering out "full;" the oldest went to sleep there. Though rich-voiced and liked, this time he retired in silence, for the audience was tormented with impatience.

The orchestra struck up a fashionable waltz, and, as the door, at the back of a drawing-room scene, was opened in both flaps by the liveried servants, a young lady entered, so fresh, delightful and easy that for a moment it seemed as if it were a member of the "highest life" who had blundered off the street into this strange world.

ALEXANDRE DUMAS, FILS

From her glistening hair of gold to the tip of her white satin slippers, with preposterously high heels, this was the new incarnation of the woman who ends the Nineteenth Century. She was indisputably beautiful, and Claudius, who had thought that the Jewess was incomparable, feared that the apple would have to be halved, since neither could have borne it entire away. But the Jewess's loveliness exalted the beholder; this one's was of the strange, irritating sort, resisted with difficulty and alluring a man into those byways which end in the gaming hell, the saturnalian halls, and the suicide's grave. Love had never chosen a more appetizing form to be the pivot on which human folly—perhaps human genius—was to spin idly and uselessly, like a beetle on a pin in a naturalist's cabinet.

Kaiserina von Vieradlers was the modern Venus, a creation of the modiste rather than of the sculptor; though hips and bosom were developed extravagantly, the long waist was absurdly small; but no token of ill health from the tight lacing appeared in the irreproachable shape, the well-turned arms and the countenance which was unmarred in a single lineament; the movements were not strictly ladylike, they were too unfettered in spite of the smooth gloves and the stylish unwrinkled ball dress, rather short in front to parade the slippers mentioned and silk stockings so nicely moulded to the trim ankle as to show the dimple. She was more fair in her eighteenth year—if she were so old—than a Danish baby in the cradle. The yellow hair had a clear golden tint not tawny, and the fineness was remarkable of the stray threads that serpentined out of the artistic braid and drooping ringlets. The blue eyes had a multitude of expressions and gleams; now hard as the blue diamond's ray, now soft as the lapis lazuli's glow of azure; the expression was at present one of longing, tender, cajoling and coaxing—like a gentle child's, never refused a thing for which it silently pleaded.

The costume was a trifle exaggerated, as is allowable on the minor stage, but what was that in our topsy-turvy age, when the disreputable woman in a mixed ball is conspicuous among her spotless sisters by the quiet correctness of her toilet?

Kaiserina came down to the flaring footlights, after a little trepidation, which the inexorable demon of stage-fright exacted from her, with the swing and confident step of one sure that—while man may be unjust, cruel and oppressive to her sex off the stage—here she would reign and finally triumph. She bowed her head, but it was to acknowledge her gracious acceptance of the tribute of applause; she moistened her fiery-coal lips with a serpent's active tongue; she surveyed her dominion with eyes that assumed a passing emerald tint. There was a depth to those apparently superficial glances. It seemed to Claudius that one had singled him out, and he fancied, as his eyes became fastened on this vision of concentrated worldly bliss, that it was for him that she stretched her plump neck, waved her arms in long gloves, undulated her waist and murmured—though to others she was but repeating her song during the orchestral prelude:

"You talk of plunging into the strife; you are ready to endure privations, you would study and toil till you vanquish. Nonsense; you had far better repose, recruit after the humdrum, exhaustive life of college; enjoy life a little. Hear a love-song, not a professor's lecture— see a dance of the ballet, not the procession of the deans and proctors; come to me for I am immediate sensation—the pleasure for all times— eternal intoxication—certain oblivion—the ideal bliss of the Hindoo! I am the grandest proof of Life—I am Love embodied!"

What did she sing to the strains of the voluptuous-waltz made vocal? The words mattered not; in Esquimaux they would have been as intelligible from the intonation with which she imbued every note, and the restricted but perfectly comprehensible gestures with which she emphasized the phrases of double meaning—one for the literary censors who had "passed" this corruption, the other for even the more obtuse of the common herd.

The rival whom, without having seen her, she had dethroned, was obliterated. It was not a transfer of allegiance—it was Semiramis; trampling an overthrown empress among the charred ruins of her palace, acclaimed without one dissentient shout, in her stead, and as the initial of a new line of sovereigns. She enchanted, interested and amused, while Rebecca had awed, ravished and strove apparently in vain to lift to a level where the élite alone soar without dread of a fall.

A witty cardinal has said that if a fly were seen in the drinking-cup by an Italian, a Frenchman and a German, respectively, the first would send it away, the second fish out the insect before he drank, while the German would gulp liquor and fly, without demur.

The good audience of Freyers' Harmonista swallowed the so-called Fraulein von Vieradlers, flies and all! Claudius saw no more clearly than they; not only was the girl an unsurpassable idol, but to its very feet it was pure gold and immaculate ivory. An insane idea seized him not only to win her—a hundred around him shared that desire—but to keep her spotless, as he thought her, whatever the gossips had said. After all, slander had no opening to attack one whose youth was manifest; who owed no complexion to the wax-mask, the bismuth powder, and the carmine; whose hair was real and fine and of a shade which no dye could imitate; and whose movements, though in a society dance far removed from the wild whirl of the monads seen on this same stage, had the freedom of the bacchantes.

After all, the unworthiness of the object no more changes the quality of love than that of the glass alters the banquet of wine.

Oh, to withdraw her from this turbulent career, for which surely she was not inextricably destined, and let her be the bright but flawless ornament of a happy home and a choice circle—if not the lady of fashion, in case the student realized one of his fantastic dreams of aimless ambition. The quiet learner felt an immense flame usurp the place of his blood; he seemed gifted with the powers of the athletic Duke of Munich, Christopher the Leaper, whose statue adorned the proscenium, and like him, clearing the orchestra with a bound of twelve feet, he would have grasped the girl wasting her graces of voice and person on these boors, and carried her off to a more congenial sphere.

Obliged to repeat her song and the dance which filled the gap between two verses, the charmer held the spectators in a spell even more firm than that she had first imposed.

No one was conscious at the first that down the central aisle had come a little party odd enough in its components and awe-inspiring in what might be called its rear-guard to break even enchantment more potent.

An old woman, wearing over sordid garments an old furred Polish pelisse, was the guide—the herald, so to say, to a gentleman in gold spectacles and a black suit and silk hat, an inspector of police, a sergeant of the watch, while behind this formidable official nucleus marched a serried body of civil and of military police. After them all, wringing his fat hands, trotted the proprietor, with a terrified expression too great not to be assumed. Waiters completed the retinue, wearing faces much whiter than the napkins slung on their arms.

As the orchestra faced the audience, they perceived this inroad before the latter and, as by a signal, ceased playing. The startled dancer, for all her aristocratic self-command, stopped immediately for explanation, and, riveting her glances on the female head of the intruders, whom she recognized—that was clear—stood stupor-stricken.

Claudius, following her hint, turned to the center and had no difficulty in recognizing in the woman arrayed in the Polish pelisse, the chief of the beggars, Baboushka. He recalled the remark of the Jew, that she befriended this debutante, and he was averse to believing it. That delicious creature and this hideous one in ties of communion! ridiculous, monstrous!

Spite of his concern for himself, Claudius noticed that twenty or thirty of the spectators, apparently perplexed at the rare conjunction of their leader and the authorities in friendly communication, would not wait for the elucidation but began to make a rush for the outlets.

The voice of the town inspector, rotund and sonorous, froze them with terror, although not personal.

"Gentlemen—(the ladies were apparently here only on sufferance, and the stage-performer was of no consideration in the authorities' eyes)—Gentlemen, a murder has been committed and we seek the culprit here in your midst!"

"Murder!" and the audience rose to their feet like one man.

"Stand up here," said the functionary, pointing to a place on a bench which a timid spectator had vacated, and pushing Baboushka roughly, "and point out the man who has made away with the honorable Major von Sendlingen."

"Major von Sendlingen!" repeated the audience, shocked, as the officer had been seen but the night previously among them in lusty life, and death is a spectre most terrible in a saloon of mirth and carousal.

After that general exclamation, a silence ensued; one that meant acquiescence in the proceedings of the police.

"I must have killed him," thought the student. "This is a black prospect! I had better have quitted the hall and profited by the invitation of refuge which Herr Daniels offered me."

For the moment, he could take no part, though he could not doubt that Baboushka would denounce him—a stranger, and the principal in the duel with canes. His cloak would help toward the identification and unless the hag's crew had abstracted it, it would be forthcoming, he doubted not.

Indeed, elevated on her perch, able to see the faces of all around her, the hag's aged but brilliant eyes rapidly scanned those nearest her in wider and wider circles. All at once they became fixed upon Claudius, and by instinct, the neighbors fell away from him so that he was isolated. She extended her arm with an unnatural vigor, and in a voice also unexpectedly strong with malice, cried:

"That is he! there you have the slayer of poor Major von Sendlingen!"

At that very moment, a shrill, ear-splitting whistle sounded; and the gas-jets all over the hall went out too simultaneously for the act not to be that of a hand at the inlet from the street-main. Claudius heard the soldiers and policemen buffeting the people to scramble over the benches toward him. He had but a single road to a possible escape: by the little door in the wall through which Rebecca Daniels had ushered him into the auditorium. He stooped as he turned, to elude any outstretched hands, drove himself like a wedge through the compacted mass of frightened spectators and, spite of the gloom, the deeper because of the glare preceding it, he reached the egress. The uninitiated would never have suspected its existence, for the actors and staff of the establishment alone had the right and knowledge to use it.

"Lights, lights!" the functionaries were shouting.

By the time matches were struck and lanterns brought into the scene of confusion, Claudius had opened the panel, leaped through and closed it. He did not dally in the passage, but hastened to follow the walled-in road as well as he might by which he had penetrated the theatrical region.

At the dividing-line, where the path parted to the men's and to the ladies' dressing-rooms, he perceived a ghostly figure in the obscurity which also prevailed here from the general extinction of the illuminant. He was about shrinking back and fleeing in another direction when eyes blazed in the dark like a cat's, and the sweet, unmistakable voice of the singer, who had enthralled him, exclaimed:

"As God lives, it is you!"

"Suppose it is I!" he returned, impatiently. "Stand aside, or—"

"You must not pass here!" she returned, laying her hands on his lifted arm.

"Must not? We shall see about that!" and he repulsed her violently.

"No, no; you are too hasty! I mean that would be a fatal course. Here, here!" seizing him again and dragging him with her. "You were right to kill that ruffian! to cane him to death—like the Russian grand-dukes, he was not born to die by the sword. To abduct one woman while paying court to another, the traitor! But, never heed that! He is punished, and you must be saved. Here is an outlet: pursue the passage to the end and leave the town!"

"But I—"

"How can you repay me? Bah! repay me in the other world—below, with a drop of cold water when I parch!" And with a dulcet yet demoniacal laugh, the singular creature pushed him into a lightless lobby, slammed a door and seemed to run away, singing the refrain of the waltz which was to haunt him forever-more.

V

Under Munich

After an instant's reflection in the impenetrable shades, Claudius concluded to follow the advice of the variety theatre's prima donna. While a stranger to the City of Breweries, he knew that its predestination toward thirst was due to its being the site of an ancient rock-salt mine. In other cities, subterraneans were melodramatic; here, a labyrinth under the surface and at the level of the dancing and drinking cellars was so natural that a child of Munich, dropped into a well, would have no misgivings as to his worming his way up into the outer air.

At the worst, when pressed by hunger, he could no doubt make an appeal to the mounted patrol by night or the foot-passengers by day, whom he would hear overhead, and be released from this living burial at the cost of the imprisonment and trial which he had temporarily evaded.

Remembering that he had a box of cigar-lights, and regretting again the want of the cloak so useful in these damp passages, he lighted a match and began his flight by the sole opening that he spied. An odor of sausages, cheese and coarse tobacco was here and there strong, and he correctly divined that at these points, fugitives, probably from the same enemy as he fled, had recently made halts. Once assured that he was in a kind of thoroughfare, though one for the nefarious, he felt bolder and more hopeful about reaching a desirable goal.

He did not pause to think, as he continued, choosing, where there was a bifurcation, the most trampled corridor, hewn originally by the miners' pick. But he had much on his mind for future elaboration. Heretofore no man could have lived a less eventful life, passed among books, globes, drawing tools and lecture notes. In a few hours the change was great. The quiet student, with no aspirations but the completion of his wandering-year in Italian picture-galleries, had become a fugitive from justice, and on the hands, groping in a lugubrious earthen alley, were the stains of a fellow-creature's blood. Then, too, the singular friendships he had formed, the old Jew and his daughter, who were awaiting him—and this still more remarkable creature who had glanced across his path, like the divinities from above in antique poems, to point out the safe retreat.

But too long a time elapsed without his finding such an evidence of his security as he had too confidently expected. He might have mistaken the true line, for while at any point of divergence there were marks in the earth, where traces of saline flows still glistened, and even stones and bits of stick placed in cavities in the manner of the gypsy clues familiar to social outcasts, he could not interpret them; for once, his university education proved faulty.

A new alarm arose from the presence of swarms of rats; larger and more hideous than their fellows of which one catches a fleeting view in houses and in the streets, they seemed to be less afraid of the lord of creation than fables teach. They scuttled off in front of him, it is true, but he began to think that they followed him when he went by. One ray of comfort came in the two beliefs that his flashing matches frightened them, and that, for certain portions of the way, well-regulated droves of the vermin had districts assigned them; those that ventured in chase of him too far were beaten back by those on whose grounds they rashly trespassed.

This latter consolation was lost almost at the same time as the other: his stock of fuses ran out, while with the last flash he feared that he saw a larger mass than ever before in his track. The rats had united to overwhelm him.

Seized with panic, spite of his philosophy, dropping the all but empty wax-light case in his haste, he dashed madly forward, groping to save his head and shoulders from contact with the capacious gallery sides, but unable to take a step with any certainty how it would end. Fortunately, he had strayed back into an often-traveled path, and while the scamper of the rats died away at the close of his frantic race, he heard a sound but little above his level revealing the presence of man. It was not a cheerful sound; being the tolling of a bell such as is swung when a dead body is entering a cemetery, is carried to the chapel before interment.

Nevertheless, fellow beings would be near and he had only to find the opening by which this burial-ground could be reached. He remembered that the old cemetery had been immensely extended, if the guide-books were to be credited, and, while he had no clear idea of the direction he had rambled, he might have reached the town of twenty thousand dead. The idea was gruesome of having to call for the aid of

ALEXANDRE DUMAS, FILS

a grave-digger, but he felt that he could not much longer support this journey in the underworld without the bodily support of food or the mental one of human fellowship.

Silence most oppressive had followed the patter of the myriad of rats' feet, and it checked his efforts. They were brought to a termination just when he looked forward with joy to a grey light dimly indicating some aperture on the other side of which shone the day. The ground seemed to give way under him, and he was hurled senseless into the pit which he had not suspected.

When he returned to consciousness, the bell had ceased to toll; the silence was once more heavy. But the pangs of hunger—remorseless master over the young—spurred him into rising.

He was thankful that he had not been attacked in his helplessness by the vermin, and he muttered a prayer in his first stride toward where he recalled the feeble light. The rats' compact column had figured in his dreams, and while they were led by the fair waltz-singer and dancer in order to devour him, unable to resist, the benignant fairy, for once dark—contrary to all precedent—wore the appearance of Rebecca.

He could not see the light; but a current of warm air stealing steadily into the underground indicated the orifice. It was a welcome draft, for it differed in many features from the noisome, dank and earthy exhalations to which he had luckily become accustomed in his indefinite sojourn.

His surmise was correct. Through a grating of iron bars, straight at the side and semi-circular at the top, set in massive masonry of some building, in the foundation of which he crouched, he saw, in the vagueness of clouded starlight, the domain of the dead.

On being assured of this, the panic, mastering him before, resumed its sway; it gave him a giant's strength to escape the fancied, grisly pursuers, and he moved the whole series of bars far enough away to enable him to crawl through the gap.

He stood, exhausted, panting, glad of the relief from the waking nightmare which the darkness encouraged. His weakness could be accounted for, as his wandering had lasted long; the syncope could not be brief since nearly thirty hours must have transpired from his rush out of the variety music-hall.

Before him, for at his back stood the chapel for services, stretched out the vast cemetery. Some of the cracked, dilapidated tombs dated back to 1600; others marked the addition in 1788 to the original God's-acre. All was hushed; it was difficult to imagine a phantom where neglect seemed to rule. It was not in this olden part that descendants of the departed flocked on All Saints' Day to decorate the mausoleums with evergreens, plaster images and artificial immortelle garlands. Except for a screeching-sparrow, which his first steps dislodged, not a sign of life appeared in this town around which the living city slept as quietly.

His eyes clearing, he believed he descried the gateway and, sure that so large a *campo santo* would have a warder in hourly attendance, he made his way, deviating as the tombs compelled, toward the entrance. To his surprise, all was still there, and though a lamp burned in the little stone lodge, it was certainly untenanted. The gate was ajar; there was no fear of the tenants flitting out bodily for a night's excursion.

Claudius was dying for refreshment and he was not fastidious about intruding. A man who has traversed the underlying catacombs need not be delicate about taking a nip of spirits or a hunch of bread. Both were in a cupboard in the little domicile, supplied with a porter's chair so ample as to be the watcher's bed, and a stove where a fire merrily burned, crackling with billets of pine wood.

The disappearance was the more strange, as on a framed placard, at the base of which was a row of brazen knobs, there was a formal injunction for the gatewarder never to go away without his place being taken by another "from sunset to sunrise and an hour after!"

Claudius knew what those knobs and the instructions portended in this adjunct to the charnel house. The public mortuary was at the other end of the wires from those bells; the custom was to attach them to the dead so that, if their slumbers were not that knowing no waking and they stirred even so little as a finger, the electric transmitter which they agitated would sound the appeal.

And now the watcher, on whom perhaps depended the duration of a worthier life than his, had paltered with his trust, while drinking at the beer-house or chattering with a sweetheart, the bell might ring unheeded, and the unhappy creature, falling with the last tremor of vitality, to obtain a desperate succor, would become indeed the corpse like which he had been laid out in the morgue.

Claudius smiled grimly and sadly. On what flimsy bases the best plant of wise men too often rest! The latest power of nature had been harnessed to do man service in his utmost extremity; science had perfected its instruments, but one link in the chain was fallible man. The bell would tinkle—the watcher would be laughing out of earshot— and the life would sink back into Lethe after swimming to the shore!

ALEXANDRE DUMAS, FILS

The student sighed as he ate the piece of bread broken off a small loaf and drank from the bottle out of which the faithless turnkey hobnobbed with the sexton, the undertaker's men and the hearse-coachman.

If the bell should ring, with him alone to hear, ought he hasten out by the gate providentially open, and leave for the care of heaven alone the unknown wretch who would have summoned his brother-Christians most uselessly? The resuscitated man would not be "of his parish," since he was a wanderer from afar. Let the natives bury their own dead!

At this instant, when philosophy pointed out to the student the unbarred portals, the bell in the midst of the row rang clearly if not very loudly. It sounded in his ear like the last trump. Could he doubt that this appeal was to him exclusively? The removal of the custodian, his own miraculous escape—all pointed to this conclusion.

But might he not run out and, if he saw the traitorous warder on his road, repeat to him the alarm? Not much time would be lost, for the gong still vibrated, and his personal safety ranked above his neighbor's in such a crisis.

But Claudius' hesitation had been that of physical weakness; confronted in this way with the problem of fraternity, he did not waver any longer. On the threshold of safety, he turned straight back into the jaws of destruction. He had not emerged from that darkness and depth of earth, to descend into a lower profundity and a denser darkness of the soul.

He glanced at the brazen monitor: its surface still shivered, though his senses were not fine enough to hear the faint sound. But there was no delusion; the dead in the morgue had signaled to the world on whose verge it was balanced.

It cost the student no pang now to retrace the steps he had painfully counted, to reach the building, out of the cellars of which he had so gladly climbed. On thus facing it, he knew by a window being lighted that his goal was there.

He had found fresh energy in his mission, rather than the scanty refreshment, and in three minutes was at the door. Heavy with iron banding the oak, it was not made for the hand of the dying to move it, but Claudius dragged it open with violence. He sprang inside with the vivacity of a bridegroom invading the nuptial chamber, although here was no agreeable sight.

A long plain hall, of grey stone, the seams defined with black cement; all the windows high up, small and grated; only the one door, never locked. Two rows of slate beds, three of which only were occupied; two men and a boy, nude save a waistcloth; over their heads—sluggishly swayed by the air the new-comer had carelessly admitted—their clothes were hung like shapeless shadows. They had been dredged up in the Isar's mud, found at a corner, dragged from under a cartwheel. No one identifying them, they were deposited here; their fate? dissection for the benefit of science, and interment of the detached portions in the pauper's hell.

Which had rung the bell?

Claudius investigated the three: the boy had been crushed by the sludge-basket of the steam-dredge; not a spark of life was left there, his companion was green and horrible; he, too, had passed the bourne.

But on the other row, alone, a robust man with disfigured face, and red whiskers, looked like a fresh cut alabaster statue. Cold had blanched him; but a faint steam arose from his armpits, in the sepulchral light of a green-shaded gas-jet. There heat remained to prove that the great furnace in the frame had not ceased to be fed.

The student bent over him to feel the heart, when, as promptly, he sprang back. Spite of the maltreated face, he recognized his combatant in the duel with canes; it was Major Von Sendlingen, who had been flung on the slab in the public dead-house.

Had Baboushka commanded his death to prevent her complicity in the assault on Daniels and his daughter being published, and had she suggested the stripping which caused the police to confound the noble officer with the victim of the "pickers-up" of drunkards?

But the major shivered in the blast from the door left open, and a brief flush ran over the icy skin.

If his enemy did not extend relief to him immediately, he would never recover strength to ring the death-bell to which ran the wires appended to his fingers and toes.

With three or four rapid strokes and twistings, Claudius broke them. He looked round; this waif of the gutter had no clothes, but a torn and shapeless garment dangled over his head; it was the old cloak of the student. The pockets had been torn bodily away to save time; it was the mere integument of the garment.

But it sufficed to retain the scanty heat lingering in the unfortunate man, when wrapped about him. With a surprising spell of strength, Claudius lifted him upon his breast when so enveloped, and crossed the grounds for the third time.

The warder had returned but he had left the gate open to close its sliding grate by mechanism worked within his little house. To his amazed eyes, Claudius presented himself with the burden.

"Help him! revive him! he is living!" he said. "I will go fetch the police surgeon! it is my officer—Major von Sendlingen!"

After the announcement of the rank, Claudius knew that the officer would want for nothing. He let the body fall into the large armchair and, taking advantage of the warder's consternation at seeing the dead-like body sitting between him and the only exit, glided through the narrow space between the sliding rails and disappeared.

The boom of an alarm bell, set swinging over the gateway by the warder, added wings to his feet, for he feared that police and patrol would hurry to the cemetery from all quarters, and he wanted, above all, to reach the Jew's hotel before morning.

VI

Two Augurs

Fortunately for the student, the night birds whom he met and to whom in asking information to arrive at the Persepolitan Hotel, he gave preference over the policemen, felt a fellow feeling for a man pallid, tottering, and in clothes which had suffered during his scramble through the exhausted mines underlaying Munich.

He reached the hotel before dawn and was not sorry to find it one of those old-fashioned hostelries continuing traditions of the posting-houses, where he might not expect to be challenged because of his appearance. In the stable yard, between a half-awakened horse and a sleepy watchdog, who received the new guest with a blinking eye and affectionate tongue, an ostler was washing down a ramshackle chaise. Claudius guessed that it was prepared for his flight and his heart warmed at this proof of the Jew having counted on his coming, though belated. The shock-headed man, clattering over the rounded stones in wooden shoes, made to fit by the insertion of straw around his naked feet, no sooner heard him name Herr Daniels as the one expecting him, than he bade him welcome in a cordial tone which his surly face had not presaged.

"I suppose he is asleep," he said, "but he left word that he was to be aroused at any hour on your coming. I am not allowed within doors in my stable dress," he added, "but you will have no trouble in finding the rooms. It is that one where the candle burns, one floor above, numbers 11, 12 and 13—the number is unlucky for a Christian, but that does not matter for the likes of them!—and a lamp burns at the turn of the stairs. The back door is on the latch."

Claudius, with the satisfaction of having anchored in the harbor, crossed the yard and entered the house. He was closing the door behind him when he heard a heavy tread at the street gate where he had come in. and the dog began to growl. The ostler caught it by the collar as it made a bound, and cried out:

"Who is there?"

The schutzman, who had dismounted, prudently held the door close, with one hand, to prevent the dog gliding through, while he showed his sword drawn in the other, and answered with affected joviality:

ALEXANDRE DUMAS, FILS

"What, Karlchen, am I not known by you better than by your pagan of a hound? But catch me putting silly questions to my boon-companion, my oldest friend! It is not in here that I saw a suspicious shadow creep, eh?"

"By my faith!" replied the groom, laughing heartily, "it may have been a shadow—but flesh-and-blood is what my true Ogre is waiting for! We are up betimes, worthy Hornitz, and we have neither had our breakfast. What has put you on the alert?"

"A general order! There was a riot at the great music hall of the Freyers Brothers—plague on it! What art they have in brewing beer that leaves a pleasant memory! and we have orders to overhaul every suspicious character in the streets, while none can get out of the town. It appears that some monstrous criminal is at large! Oh, for the reward, that would buy me a little cottage on the Friedplatz road with beer unstinted!"

"Pooh! as usual, you gentlemen of the nightwatch are badly informed," grumbled the ostler, pushing the dog into a corner. "I know what it was, for one of the theatrical players is a lady lodger of ours. She was unfairly supplanted by some insignificant young upstart and, of course, the public, always knowing true talent from shallow pretension, broke up the seats and pelted the manager with it along with his imposter!"

"Well, good-morning, Karlchen," said the gendarme, taking the correction in good part, and withdrawing his booted leg from the door. "I may see you when I am off duty and we will make sure that Freyers have better taste in brewing beer than in choosing actresses."

Having heard enough to convince him that Daniels was in a house guarded by the faithful, Claudius proceeded up the stairs dimly visible before him at the end of a clean, bricked passage. His progress was more easy when he reached the landing, as the lamp mentioned, in a recess and projecting its rays in two directions, shone on the door of the suite of three rooms where the Jew and his daughter were lodged.

Pausing before he knocked, Claudius heard the soft step of slippered feet. On tapping discreetly, a reserved voice ordered him to come in. It was Daniels who spoke; he was in a dressing-gown, with bare head, and, having cleared the chairs back to enable him to make the circuit of the table in the center of the spacious room, had apparently been walking round it like a caged lion. On the table were various articles heaped up without order and an open trunk, partly packed. He looked up in emotion while Claudius paused on the sill, more affected than he understood the reason for.

"Ah, heaven be praised! it is you," said the old man with grave joy, and holding out his hands, paternally. "I feared for the worst—that you would never come. It is so serious a matter: a nobleman and an officer who belongs to the Secret Intelligence Department—his death is not to go unpunished."

"At least, he is not dead," said the student; and he hastened to tell his story.

"Speak at any tone you please," interrupted Daniels, at the stage of his having escaped from the music-hall by the artistes' door and of the help of the woman whom he did not profess to distinguish. "My daughter is sleeping, and a sitting-room is here between her apartment and this one."

But, though without any fear that the noble girl would stoop to listen, the student related the rest with a cautious voice. Others might not be so delicate.

"You have a great heart," said Daniels, when he heard of the rescue of the major from the frigid slab of the morgue. "To do this for an enemy is lofty conduct. God grant that you have not met one of those monsters of ingratitude whom a kind act embitters. But it would hardly appear that he could survive the beating by Baboushka's gang, the ill usage from the street sweepers and that of the ghouls of the dead-house. All this makes me tremble for the plan I formed to have you conveyed hence in a chaise. I have the papers to cover your departure as a clerk whom a business firm of good standing are sending out to Buenos Ayres. Once at Hamburg, you may turn your face in any direction you desire. But the slayer of Major Von Sendlingen would not be able to cross the French or Italian frontier."

"For a man intending to see Italy, that would be taking me greatly out of the road," muttered Claudius, sinking into a chair.

"Then go as far as Ulm only, where you will let the train proceed without you. Send for a doctor whose address I will give you and I answer for his helping you to get into Switzerland. After all, that will be better. But I see that you are weak with your exertions and want of proper nourishment."

"It is rest I most need."

"Then stretch yourself on this sofa, and let me cover you with a traveling-rug. When you awake, refreshments will be at hand."

ALEXANDRE DUMAS, FILS

"But you, whom I deprive of rest?"

"It is true that anxiety about you, my young friend, has prevented me lying down, but I am not desirous of sleep now. Do as I tell you. I will countermand the chaise, and return with the food. This house is not a famous inn, but my coreligionists, who are traveling merchants, frequent it, and the edibles are good. As for the honesty of the servants and of the host, I guarantee it. Unless you have been dogged to the door, I believe you are safe."

Claudius said that he seemed not to have been followed. At the house, a patrolman had caught a glimpse of him but the ostler had jestingly turned him off and quieted his suspicions. Before his host had reached the door, where he paused to look back, the young man was nodding with eyes closing in spite of his will, and he was soon steeped in slumber.

"The sleep on the night before execution," muttered the Jew. "This is a sad matter! That Baboushka is a witch of malevolence, or I am woefully misinformed, and the major an awkward antagonist. I would a thousand miles separated my daughter, and this young man, from both of them."

In the lobby he saw a young girl, with her hair in curl-papers and a candle in her hand, descending the stairs from above.

"Ah, Hedwig," he said gently, "I am not sorry you have risen so early." The girl blushed.

"You are as rosy as a carnation. Will you please bring me up some coffee and light food as soon as you get the hot water? My daughter and I will probably start before your regular breakfast-hour."

The girl seemed vexed by this news, for she bit her lip, but forcing a smile, she continued her journey to the kitchen. No one else seemed afoot in the large and rambling house, through which the Jew sent searching looks as he took the turn to the yard. The ostler received him with a grin, and the dog with friendly wags of the stub tail.

"We shall not use the chaise as we purposed, Karl," said the Jew. "At your breakfast-time, my daughter will go out alone for an airing, with you or your fellow to drive. The young gentleman whom you welcomed is quite unfit for a journey before at least three days are over. Meanwhile, not an incautious word that will betray where he took shelter. In these three days," he added to himself, "we shall know how the major fares. Unfortunately, his race have iron constitutions."

This was said with a sorrow rare in one of a people who seldom deplore the survival of a brother man.

Daniels was right in his fear: the student needed repose, and only the most vigorous counter measures drove off an attack of fever. Rebecca was his nurse in the same devoted and intelligent manner as her father was his physician, but as he was on the margin of delirium half the time, he saw her like one in a vision.

His antagonist, Von Sendlingen, was not so blessed. After a cursory treatment in the cemetery gate-keeper's lodge, he was removed, wrapped in blankets, to his quarters in the great barracks; the iron constitution, of which Daniels spoke, bore him up, and before Claudius was on foot again, the officer was outdoors—a little pale, but seemingly none the worse for his horrible adventure.

He took up his own case. Fraulein von Vieradlers had already tired of her assay in elevating the stage in a social point of view. She had excited the adoration of the eccentric Marchioness de Latour-lagneau, a very old lady of fortune, who had the habit of conceiving singular fancies. This lady engaged the cantatrice as a "noble companion," and she hurried off with her into Italy. So the story ran, and added that her manager found that the Vieradlers promptly repudiated any kinship with her when he talked of their paying the forfeit money. He had thereupon endeavored to win back La Belle Stamboulane to his deserted stage, but she was obdurate, and the beer flowed flat in the double absence of stars inimitable.

The major, whose body, reeking with arnica and iodine, reminded him at every step of the drubbing he owed to the civilian, concentrated his searches therefore to discover him. He was sure that he had not left the town by the ordinary channels, but, as time passed, and the week ended fruitlessly, he was inclined to believe that the fiend which befriended Baboushka had also shielded Claudius with his wing.

He did not doubt that the old hag, believing he was lifeless, had hounded on her followers to steal his uniform and hurl him into the kennel for the most hideous of fates, which even the homeless and hopeless dread. But for the enemy whom he hated, he might now be a boxful of dissected bones in the poor man's lot instead of still enjoying the prospect, dear to the scion of an ancient race, of occupying his shelf in the family vault.

Although a soldier, he had such intimate relations with the civil powers, that the police aided him in searches which he took care astutely to represent as quite non-personal. They led him to the street of the Persepolitan Hotel, where, before he entered, he was scrutinizing the vicinity when he spied the well-known form of the old beggar-chief. Their surprise was alike.

"Traitress!" he said, with a red spot blazing on his pale cheeks, as he played with the swordknot on his new sword as if he wanted to loose it and flog her. "After receiving my gold, to bring me to death's door! What have you to say to stay me from handing you to the town's officers to be whipped out of it at the cart's-tail?"

To his surprise again, she met his glance firmly, and her eyes seemed as irate as his own.

"You are mistaken," she replied, carelessly, as if the matter were of no consequence. "How can you expect those stalwart bullies to obey an old woman like me? They would have beaten me to a jelly if I had tried to shield you. Besides, my officer, I thought you had not a spark of life left in you after that beating."

"He shall pay for it—with the sword if worthy—with the stick if a plebeian."

"You need not believe he will ever meet you with the sword," said the hag, glad to have the dialogue turn on another head than her own in spite of her unconcern. "I am going to tell you all about one whom I hated by instinct and whom I find to be a hereditary enemy."

"What do you mean? He is but a boy and cannot have wronged you or yours."

"His father, major, murdered my loveliest daughter and interrupted her career of splendor! Alas! one that had a palace where kings were received and to whom princes often sued in vain!"

"Halloa! you, to have a daughter of that calibre!" and he laughed coarsely.

"You, who know everything, my officer, must at least have heard of the peerless Iza, the original of the most beautiful statue which—reproduced in the precious and the mean metals, in clay, in parian, in plaster—made the round of the civilized world? 'The Bather!' That was my daughter! She had her faults—even the truly lovely have mental flaws, though bodily they are perfect—but whilst she lived, her poor old mother dressed in silks and velvets—not in rags; she ate and drank delicately, not sour crusts and sourer wine; she slept on down and not in a cellar!"

Von Sendlingen shook his head; he was of the new generation and he preserved but a dim remembrance of the noted beauties—the stars of the living galaxy decorating the first cycle of the Bonapartist Restoration.

"I foresaw it all and I warned her; but she was so perverse! It is my duty to avenge her, and to see that the same blunder is not made by— no matter! Enough that my science—at which you smile, I see—points out to me that your greatest enemies and mine are in that house." She gestured toward the hotel, which the major had been studying.

"Do you say enemies in the plural?" he said, ceasing to curl his lip in mocking of the witch.

"In that house are the Jewish couple, father and daughter, who played at the Harmonista, La Belle Stamboulane and the Turkophonist Daniel, and the young man who belabored your excellency so that he almost died of the drubbing."

"Hang you for being so profuse in your explanations! How do you know all this?"

"The servant-maid is a customer of mine. I tell her fortune and she tells me all that goes on in her master's house. The young man has been cared for there these five or six days, and they only await the chance to smuggle him out of the city. Have him seized and secure him in prison, where he shall rot—for I declare to you, as surely as there are stars above, these letters of the divine volume in which soothsayers read, he will be your death in the end unless you are his."

"I would not be contented with that. I want to return him blow for blow—and yet you say I cannot fight him in duello."

"Listen, my officer. He has been brought up in ignorance of his name and origin, in my country Poland. He is French by birth, and his name is Felix Clemenceau. It was his father, a celebrated sculptor, who married my daughter Iza, after decoying her to Paris from her mother's side, and he murdered her on some frivolous pretext when they were living separated and he, heaven knows, had no farther claim upon her— his existence was pure indifference to her. I answer for it! They tried his father for the atrocity. Even a French jury could not find extenuating circumstances for that kind of cold-blooded assassin who slays in the small hours the wife of his bosom—after having cast her off and driven her to evil ways, poor, spotless angel! They brought him in guilty of a foul murder and he was guillotined—gentleman and artist of merit though he was. They were kind to his young son; his friends made up a purse and sent him afar to be educated and reared in ignorance. But the shadow of the guillotine is projected afar, and I saw its red finger point to the assassin's offspring. I have found him. If my hand is not too feeble to strike, it may anticipate yours."

"I cannot measure swords with a felon's son!" muttered Von Sendlingen. "But I shall not cease aching in the heart until he is in the shameful grave he imprudently snatched me from."

"You are a man after my own liking," said the hag, chuckling. "I can foresee that you will go far and perish in a blaze of glory! Listen! There are troublous times when an unscrupulous and ambitious soldier may make his mark and carve a good slice out of the great, rich cake called Europe. Aid me, and I will aid you. Yes, Herr Major, it is one potentate speaking with another," the singular woman went on with sinister pride, and trying to draw her shrunken form into straightness; "I rule an army of my own, camped by cohorts in the capitals of Europe— dating farther back than your own, and, perhaps, as formidable. It is we who spy out the weak spots in great cities. The next time, we shall swarm into the doomed city in a mass and we shall devour its wealth and luxuries until we are gorged. But for the day, it will be glut enough for me to have the life's blood of this man. You cannot honor him with single combat, it appears. Then, let me propose another mode to finish him."

The major was silent. Standing high in the ranks of the police, he was not sure how closely he might ally himself with this avowed leader of the evil-doers, who announced the pillage of a metropolis. She took his silence for consent or approval, for she jauntily continued:

"The house-maid has told me all they are hatching. They have a chaise always ready and passports to mask the departure of the young man as a clerk going abroad. But for precaution, they will not have him go to the train at the depot; he might be questioned and the discrepancies in the passport be perceived. The chaise is to convey him down the line, and he will get on the cars at a rural depot where the gendarme and ticket-seller will be dull and easily hoodwinked."

"Very neat," said Von Sendlingen, appreciating the plan at its due value. "I always said old Daniels was no fool."

"What more easy than to post a couple of the horse patrol on the road—young, hot-headed fellows with restless fingers on the triggers? The youth will certainly refuse to surrender, whereupon, bang, bang! he falls into the ditch with a brace of bullets in his body. You and I will have an enemy the less. This is not the way I planned it in my dreams, but we must take our revenge with the sauce fate serves it up to us 'on the table of Fact.'"

"The scheme is plausible."

"Feasible! especially will it work like well-oiled machinery if you play your part of lure creditably."

"My part?" questioned the major.

"Yes, yours. With a sorrowful eye and a smooth face, I confess I could not confront the man I hate as strongly as his father. You are different—you are an arch-villain—a born diplomatist who wears the very mask for this task and has no face, no compunction, no pity of his own. Go into that house, ask for Herr Daniels—that is the Jew player's non-professional name—and see him and his daughter, perhaps, the young student, too. Boldly proclaim your position as the Secret Intelligence Agent, by which you learned their whereabouts, and that they harbor the charitable young man who saved your life. Touch lightly on his thumping you within an inch of it, and enlarge on your undying gratitude. Apologize to the young lady—lay all blame on her irresistible charms and abuse a little the fair and fickle Fraulein von Vieradlers who has eloped without so much as an adieu to you! Depend upon it, Jews though they are, they will applaud your Christian forgiveness, and, I do not doubt, Frenchman though he is, young Clemenceau will give you his hand. Dilate not at all, but urge him to leave the town without delay. From the maid I will get to know the hour of the chaise's starting and the route so that you can plant your men. I grant that this has the air of a highwayman's attack, but, after all, the uniform covers a host of civil sins, and, really, I do not see a better way to have done with the youth. It will never do to have him strut about Paris boasting that he snatched the sword away from an officer and drubbed him with a cane into the bargain."

Sullen fire burned in the hearer's eyes. He stamped his foot, suppressed an oath, and when he looked up, had a serene countenance.

"You have said enough. A willing steed does not need the spur. I will lay the train and prepare the match. Let each look to himself lest he suffer by the explosion."

Successful though the old woman had been in her arrangement to convert an offended employer into a vigorous ally, she shuddered as if he were, in these ominous words, as good a soothsayer as he pretended to be.

VII

One Good Turn Deserves—A Bad One

Probably no more terrifying a figure could have presented itself at the Persepolitan Hotel than the major of cavalry, and he looked the type of his class, insolent with aristocratic hauteur, martial to the point of arrogance, and domineering and as blustering toward inferiors as he would have been bland and meek to his superiors. The landlord, one of the hybrid Levantines in whose blood that of a dozen races flowed, was as alarmed as the maid, whom he sent up the stairs to announce the visitor to Herr Daniels. Strange to say, the officer, who had taken a seat in the sitting-room, unasked, with his heavy sabre held upright between his knees, bore the somewhat lengthy delay with patience. The girl returned to say that Herr Daniels would be honored with the visit, although, he had said, he had not a pleasant remembrance of the gentleman. In fact, before his assault in the street upon La Belle Stamboulane, the major had persecuted her and deserved the reproof from her father which it was too dangerous, as Munich society was ruled, for him to utter.

But, contrary to all precedent, the military Lovelace quietly walked into the room where Claudius was restored to health and whence he had been removed to the inmost chamber vacated by the young singer. The major's accident might account for his meekness, but his manners and voice accorded with his speech so that one attributed the change to an altogether different cause than a purely physical one.

He approached the Jew with open countenance, wearing a chastened and subdued expression, and extended his hand as to a brother officer. Daniels accepted it, struck by the unexpected mien, although he could not, in his astonishment and inveterate prudence, return the pressure. The major spoke an apology for his outrageous conduct, in a faltering voice and with moist eyes, spacing the apparently unstudied phrases with a cough as if to master tearfulness unbecoming even an invalid soldier. He laid the blame on the surpassing charms of the songstress who had enflamed him beyond his self-control and, partly, on the infernal French wine in which he had imprudently over-indulged at the evening's garrison officer's dinner. Had he but patriotically stuck to the beer! But that was not worth lamenting now. He tendered his regrets to the father of the young lady and promised to use his poor influence—here he smiled at the disparagement as if he knew his power and that his hearer was sure of it—for her professional advancement as long as she rejoiced Munich with her beauty and accomplishments.

The night in the dead-house, on the very brink of the deathpit, had transformed him, he freely acknowledged. He hardly recognized his own voice in communicating the sentiments that carried him into new directions, so strange was it all, but he was eager to show by deeds that his conversion was great and sincere. He had engaged his protection for the distinguished turkophone-player and his unparalleled daughter, but he felt that was enough.

"Ample," said Daniels, at last able to speak a word on the torrent of glib language momentarily pausing; "but we are going away to fulfill an engagement in Paris."

"One moment," said the major, politely lifting his hand from which he kept the buckskin gauntlet as if he meant again to shake hands with the Ishmael at their farewell. "Perhaps I cannot, then, be of service to you, but there is another to whom my assistance is of other value—nay, of the highest consequence. I am not referring to the young lady—whom Munich will be so sorry to part with and whom I do not expect to see again even to accept my excuses—but the student from the Polish University who deservedly corrected me and brought me to my sober senses—although, perhaps, he had a heavy hand." He spoke with an assumption of manly regret, which enchanted the hearer and completed his revocation of the bad opinion of the rough suitor of his daughter. Still the Jew had not laid aside all his habitual caution and he did not by word or movement betray that he had an acquaintance with his champion.

"I see that I must drop all flourishes and speak unfettered," went on the major, bluntly. "In two words, our brawl has got to the ears of the provost-marshal as well as those of the town guardians, and the search is going to be thorough for that young gentleman. I know it is absurd, and I protested against it, but the idea has penetrated their wooden heads that he is one of those tramp-students who are permeating the masses—worse, the dangerous classes—with seditious ideas, and they think he and Baboushka's gang too long lording it in the poor quarter, are hand and glove. In fact, in a day or two—perhaps now—the forces will be a-foot in uniform and in disguise to make a keen and searching inspection of the dwellings suspected of harboring the liberal-minded; and God knows that you have, Herr Daniels, chosen a veritable hot-bed! Two months ago, we arrested a Nihilist with a portmanteau full of glass bombs, luckily uncharged, in the attic upstairs; not three weeks since, two Hungarian malcontents were stopped at the door—but why enter into these details, fitter for the police than a soldier to relate? You, of course, were not told of these blots on this hotel's fame or you would have selected it as the last roof to shelter your talented daughter. It is one thing to cross swords—I mean staves—with a man, and another to guide the watchmen to clap their coarse paws on his shoulder. I have made honorable amends, I hope, to the lady and yourself, for my rudeness; as for the gallant fellow, I bear him no ill will—on the contrary! since I could wish to meet with him again, and tell him that the Great Prison of Munich is not badly constructed and promises little chance of an escape. I beg you to convey the warning to him that he must lose not one instant if he can escape beyond the walls."

Still Daniels believed it prudent, if not polite, to make no compromising admission. But the speaker was not offended. He smiled wisely, not without good humor, and offered his hand so frankly that the Jew again took it and this time slightly returned the generous pressure.

But on the way to the door, he was stopped by the entrance of Rebecca. Although she was clad in the plain garments affected by the Jewess in ordinary days, and they were in the most striking contrast with the stage flippery in which the officer had previously seen her, her loveliness was as manifest as the stars when even a fleecy cloud veils them on an autumnal eve. In her anxiety as regarded her father—or, perhaps, the student, who can tell?—she must have stooped to listening to some portion of the singular and one-sided dialogue. For she said, without any prelude:

"Herr Officer, you have acted a noble part and it would be a grief if I had not taken the occasion to accept your apology and thank you for the warning which may save the life of one who—believe me—is no longer your foe, if he had been one. I am not able to judge the greatness and loftiness of your act from your people's point of view, but I shall no longer have a mean opinion of the creed which can perform such a conversion as yours—that is, making you a true gentleman instead of leading one to believe you a heartless libertine."

She held out her hand and he took it so reverently, without haste and with tenderness, and kissed it so respectfully that her last doubt vanished—although she scarcely had the ghost of one.

He had triumphed completely, and he retired with an airy step and a heart replete with gratification.

"If he is dragged into the prison and locked up to rot in the dungeon, they will blame me the last of all," he muttered. "Heavens, how supernally beautiful she is! There are times when I think that if she and her rival occupied the scales of the balance, a butterfly's wing would turn them. My heart would be divided in their mutual favor."

With the same aerial step, he passed two or three men in threadbare suits and shabby hats, who were hovering about the Persepolitan, and who carefully exchanged glances of understanding with him. He went straight to the superintendent-inspector of police, and sat down in his cabinet to concert with him on the best way to suppress, without scandal, the dangerous emissary from ever-restless Poland, lodged in consultation with the Jew, the bugbear of the monarchies of Europe.

"Tut, tut! tell not the official that Daniels and his daughter, for the paltry lucre of the drink-halls or for artistic satisfaction, made the tour of the capitals!"

In the meantime, the "suspects," not themselves suspicious, commenced, with Rebecca a listener, upon the move counseled by the chivalrous major. It was one they had almost settled upon and they determined to put it all the sooner into execution. The post chaise was kept in a state of readiness, alike with the horse that drew it on these important occasions, a surefooted nag whose pace was better than her appearance. Claudius, to be sure, rested under the disadvantage of being a stranger to the roads, as he had traveled only upon one to enter this city—commonly accounted dull, but so far crammed with serious adventures. This blank in his topographical lore was easily filled: the bright-eyed Hedwig was to meet him at the first corner, mount into the vehicle of which the capacious hood of enameled cloth would hide her, and there pilot him in steering to the Sendling *Thur* or gate. Once in the open country, the road was plainer—in fact, he could be guided by the locomotive's smoke and whistle till he reached the little station. Even twenty miles out, the Persepolitan's landlord had acquaintances—perhaps they were brothers in some occult league— and the vehicle could be left without misgivings at any of the inns which he named.

There was nothing in this plan, so simple as to promise success, to trouble the brain, but, all the same, Claudius had a sleepless night, though he retired early to be prepared for the probably eventful morrow.

He wished to think only of Rebecca, who had added sound hints to her father's and the host's experienced advice; but, do what he could, it was another's image that haunted him. It was the winning one of the aristocratic singer. Again he beheld her matchless shape, her caressing and enthralling eyes, her supple undulations in the waltz and her shimmering golden curls. And whatever the sounds in the street, where there seemed more footfalls than before that evening, all though actual, were overpowered and formed the burden to the ghostly but delightful strains from that silvery voice. He was not only at the age to be impressionable, but he had not known one of those college amorettes which may be as innocent as a page of a scientific text-book. No woman even in the poetry had caused him to vibrate in the untouched heart-chords like this unexpected star in the firmament of beer fumes and tobacco smoke! But it was not joyous to muse upon this vision for he had no doubt that she marked a new starting-point in his life.

Did he love her, or Rebecca? They had appeared to him so closely together that he was confused. He viewed them as a double-star, without yet having the coolness to separate them. He was a man to love once only, and there is but one love. There are different phases of it as there are different lodgers in the same house; they do not know each other, but they come in and go forth by the same staircase-way.

Of this he was instinctively certain that if he loved Kaiserina, she would guide him in altogether another direction than he had looked and whither his proud and admiring professors had pointed. Enormous wealth in our days is to the monopolist, immense fame to the specialist. To rise above contestants, one must be patient, resigned, long toiling and abhorrent of the social ties which fetter one when most of the time is demanded to solve a problem, and pester one to recite the two or three letters he has learnt when he ought to study till he masters the entire alphabet. A man must immolate himself.

Oh, he had been so happy at whiles with the thought, accounted providential, that he stood alone, with no one to distract him, to impose burdens on him and to claim a right to make inroads on his precious hours. He loved the loneliness in which he sank when he stepped out of the lecture-room and the amphitheatre. He had not felt the need, which others confessed, of some one with whom to share griefs, debate enigmas and communicate projects. Since he saw Rebecca, he had, indeed, had an almost momentary glimpse of a home where a dashing woman, moving silently and airily, guarded his meditations from the external plagues. Such a woman was created to comfort, cheer and encourage if he flagged. But the love she inspired was ideal, perceived hazily during the hours when he was out of health, and divined rather than watched her tender ministrations.

The courtships are long when love is based on respect. She gave repose to the soul, not excitement to the spirit. He saw that she admired him for his courage in daring so much—more than he had fully realized—for the despised and trampled-upon, and she pitied one before whom yawned the dreadful prison which rarely lets out the political prisoner with enough life in his wrecked frame to be worth living out. But he did not see that she was truth and that he should follow her. As the sailors drive the ship toward the false beacon, near them and garish and flaring, so he thought the erratic orb brighter than the serene fixed star.

He felt ungrateful. This sneaking out of the town was ridiculous after the heroic introduction to La Belle Stamboulane. He examined a pair of pistols which the host had generously presented him with, when, after the restless night, he rose with the dawn, and he determined to use them if assailed. It is the inoffensive, quiet man who works most mischief when roused—nothing so terrible even to the wolves as the sheep gone mad. The student, having dipped his hand in blood, was now eager to be attacked on the highway by a company of unrepentant Von Sendlingens.

This was no mood, however, in which to start on a journey of possible peril. Rebecca did not appear at the breakfast table. She, too, had passed a wakeful night, but it was in prayer for the safety of the first real friend she had so far met among the Gentiles. The host looked in at the conclusion of the meal. Nothing could wear a fairer aspect. Even the hovering figures which he, for good reason, set down as spies, had become tired of their useless quest, and disappeared with the fog that floated amid the smoke of the numerous brewery chimneys.

ALEXANDRE DUMAS, FILS

VIII

A Second Defeat

The sun was well up, showing a jolly red face, which indicated that he had been passing the night in the tropics, when Claudius, having said his farewell within the hospitable house where his bill had been obstinately withheld from him, took the reins in the chaise. The grinning ostler held the unbarred door of the yard ready to open it quickly and slam it behind him. At least, he had not the host's delicacy and he had accepted his gratuity.

"Good speed, master!" he had hastily cried out as the equipage rolled out into the street.

It was deserted. The horse and vehicle aroused no curiosity where odder animals and more curiously antiquated rattletraps were also out. He traversed the town as unimpeded as a Czar environed by secret guards. The officer at the gate, yawning behind the passport which he did not trouble to read, wished him a good dinner at the rural friend's, where it was hinted he would put up, and returned into the guardroom to resume telling a dream which he wished interpreted. Since Joseph, these functionaries at the gate and in prison seem to be tormented with puzzling visions.

All had gone well but for one serious omission: Hedwig had not appeared to be taken up; yet he had not mistaken the streets laid down in the itinerary. But once outside the walls, he was forced to go slowly and foresaw the moment when he must stop. It was hazardous to inquire, for, while he was dressed, by the hotel-keeper's provision, like a citizen of Munich, he had not the speech of the residents.

In his quandary he was greatly relieved when the horse pricked up his ears and gave a whinny in a kind of recognition. Claudius glanced to the roadside gladly and hopefully, as a young, feminine figure stepped out from the cover of a post painted in stripes to indicate parish, township and other boundary marks. But although the short frock, coarse woolen stockings, cap and velvet bodice were Hedwig's Sunday clothes, sure enough, in which the student had once seen the pretty maid, this girl was no rustic slightly polished by the hotel experience.

He felt his heart melt like wax in a cast when the bronze rushes within the clay—it was Kaiserina von Vieradlers!

A strange feeling nearly mastered him! Instinct bade him run and, whipping the horse, flee at the top of speed anywhere beyond the charm of this unexpected apparition. And yet she came forward so brightly, and so frankly, and her first words were so reassuring that he was ashamed of the impulse which—he was yet to know—had all the worth of heavenly inspired suggestions.

"Herr Student!" she said sweetly, "it is fated that I shall be of service to you. Do not go farther in this course. They lie in wait for you. Luckily, I know of a cross-country lane—if you will only let me accompany you to set you right, and help me to roll some stones and logs from the mouth. It saves time, and you will baffle your foes. Oh, I know all. The faithful Hedwig, whose clothes I have borrowed, is a daughter of a tenant on my father's estate. She means well, but she has no brains for these steps out of her even tenor, and she was glad to have me replace her in her mission. Help me up!"

There was no denying her anything. The horse had appeared to greet her with pleasure, though it was probably the clothes of Hedwig that he recognized with the whinny after a sonorous sniff.

As she held out her hand, he offered his and, like a fawn clearing a hedge, she bounded up, just touched with a winged foot the iron step, and cleared the seat with a second leap. Crouching down within the hood, she began merrily but spoke with gravity before she had finished:

"Drive on after turning."

He turned the horse and vehicle. At the same moment a shrill whistle sounded in the opposite direction.

"That's the gendarmes," she said. "The watchman's horn in the old town; the military whistle without. They are keeping good guard for you—but we shall cheat them, I tell you again!"

She laughed that purely feminine laugh at the prospect of somebody being deceived.

"Take the northern fork, although you would seem to be going very different to your aim. At the lane I spoke of, stop—but I shall be at your elbow to prompt you."

The drive was resumed in this singular way; there was something piquant in not seeing his companion, her presence manifested only by her sweet breath, the slight rustling of the glazed cloth which afforded her such scanty room, and the prattle which flowed from her lips.

She was happy to serve him again; she had liked him from the first sight in the hall; they did not seem to be strangers; he was like she knew not whom, but she could swear the resemblance was perfect! She had been read such a lecture by her manager and the police sub-chief, but, pooh! what were such men but the knob on a post—the post remained and the knob was unscrewed for another to be put on every now and then. They had threatened but she was not a strolling player who feared the lock-up and the House of Correction. They would think twice before they sent a child of the Vieradlers into the Home of the Unrepentant Magdalens! and all this intermixed with snatches of song and flashes of original wit at the expense of the police and soldiers and the citizens.

And the flight into Italy with the Marchioness famous for protégés as other old ladies for keeping cats or parrots? It was true she had made her an offer and she had connived at the police being made to think she had accompanied the eccentric dame. But she had remained in Munich to help the man who was endeared to her.

Not a word about Baboushka and a fear to break the spell kept Claudius quiet on that point.

Eight minutes passed like one, when—"Stop!" she exclaimed, and was out beside him without a helping hand and upon the dusty road.

The walls had a gap here, roughly choked up by a higgledy-piggledy heap of rubbish. Fraulein von Vieradlers had attacked it before her astonished companion, also alighting, came to her aid. There was witchery in the creature, for her delicate, ungloved hands, covered with rings, tugged at the roughly hewn tree-trunks and misshapen blocks of stone without a scratch and, as her frame offered no suggestion of strength, the swiftness with which they were moved, confirmed the idea of the supernatural. As soon as he recovered from his amazement, he aided her energetically, and in an incredibly short space the two cleared a passage for the horse to scramble over and the wheels to be lifted clean across. Without pausing, they replaced the beams and boulders, and made good the breach.

"Excellent!" exclaimed the vocalist, contemplating the work. "But I am wrong to delay. We are not out of the vale of tribulation. Help me in and tan the horse's hide well! We must, without farther delay, reach the farmhouse whose red-tiled roof gleams under the lindens. Help me in, and lay on the whip!"

This drive, at redoubled speed, despite its being in broad daylight, had to the student the fascination of the gallop of the returned dead lover and Lenore in the ballad. Though never cruel before, he now spared the horse not a stroke or impatient shout, however imprudent the latter was. On the rutty, ill-kept lane the wheels bounded unevenly and the driver had hard work to keep his seat; but the girl, by a miracle of balancing, held her half-crouching, half-standing position in the *calash*, and only now and then, flung forward by a jolt, rested her hands on Claudius' shoulders. At this contact—at the sight of those roseate, dimpled hands—he was electrified and in the headlong rush he pictured himself as Phaeton, careering behind the glancing tails of the steeds of the solar chariot.

Such a pace overtasked the poor mare. At any moment now her sudden collapse after a stumble might be expected. On the other hand, the farm-house, winning-post of the race, loomed up clearly, and, luckily, the road improved a little by becoming harder and descending gradually. On one side rose a willow coppice, in the trailing branches of which a musically rippling brook was running; on the other, the ruins of a barn, which a flood had demolished.

On the knoll beyond, the haven stood, and Kaiserina smiled as she leaned her head forward so that her cheek was next his.

Again she had saved him!

No; not yet!

From both sides of the road at the hollow, three horsemen came solemnly forth, two from the right, one from the ruins.

The girl turned pale and shrank back. Claudius flung down the broken whip, and, taking the reins in his teeth, held a pistol in each hand. He had recognized in the most prominent rider Major von Sendlingen, and in an instant he comprehended that this was a trap and that his chivalric, Christian conduct was the most base of impudent tricks.

Was Kaiserina also a betrayer? He did not believe that.

Each horseman had a pistol as well as a sword drawn, and, besides, the two inferiors were armed with carbines. This had the air of an assassination, and, infuriated by the treachery, Claudius resolved to begin the attack. It mattered little whether Fraulein von Vieradlers was in the conspiracy or not. Once she had saved his life, and he was bound not to molest her now, so long as she remained neutral. She had cowered down, from fear or because her guilt oppressed her. Perhaps his contempt would punish her sufficiently.

The old mare bore the unusual exertion bravely and charged down the incline against the odds like a war-stallion.

"Take him alive!" shouted the major, beating down the pistols with his sword flat, as a second thought changed his first intention.

He had spied the young singer in the shadow of the hood, and he had no wish to injure her.

"That's not as you decide!" retorted Claudius, and he fired both shots at the same time.

But he had not allowed for the steep descent. One bullet stung the major in the thigh, the other so cruelly lacerated the horse of the gendarme on his right that it screamed, reared and fell sidewise with a crash into the brook. The man, although encumbered by his heavy boots, contrived to disengage himself and stood up, furious at being unhorsed.

At the same moment, out of the reeds, much as though the disappeared horse had suffered a transformation, an old woman leaped up into the lane. Her grey hair was disheveled and her pelisse was shredded by the brambles. She ran to place herself before the horse in the chaise and the gendarmes, and screamed, with her eyes fastened on the girl in the vehicle:

"Hold! do not shoot! God is not willing!" But the major alone obeyed the injunction; the others, in the saddle and dismounted, were wild with rage and pain. Their two firearms rang out as one, and the old woman had only time to cover the mark by drawing herself to her full height, with an effort unknown for thirty years. Both bullets entered her chest, for she fell under the horse's feet, as it stumbled and went down beside her.

As the vehicle abruptly came to a stop, quivering in every portion, Claudius clung to the frame of the hood to save himself from being cast out. The girl was hurled against him, but she did not think of herself. She thrust into his hand a revolver and whispered rapidly:

"Quick! they are going to fire again!"

It was true; excepting, this time, the gendarmes had recourse to their carbines, the dismounted one having picked his up from the briars, and found the cap secure. At that short range, the student would be a dead man if he awaited the double discharge.

Heated with the action, inhaling the acrid smell of gunpowder, the demon possessed him which at such moments hisses: "Kill, kill, kill!" into a man's ear. The angelic demon there had supplied him with the weapon, and he fired three shots as rapidly as the mechanism would work.

The dismounted gendarme had come out on an unlucky day; a bullet in his neck laid him lifeless in the rushes beside the strangled horse; his comrade, pierced so that he bled internally, drew off to the roadside mechanically—the image of despair; nothing more heartrending than the anguish on his convulsed visage and the increasingly hopeless expression.

Here was a double tragedy, but it was the major who, under the eyes of Fraulein von Vieradlers, was to furnish the comedy of the incident. His horse took the bit in its teeth and ran away with him along the bank of the brook, threatening at any moment to lose footing and roll the two in the water.

"Victory!" said the girl, with a joy-flushed cheek, alighting and displaying no more compassion for the soldiers slain in doing their duty than for the chaise horse—or the old woman beside its heaving carcass.

"She is dead," remarked Claudius. "But what did she say? She spoke in Polish—I understand it—I caught the words, but they were not intelligible."

"Were they not?" continued the girl, not displeased.

"She said, 'my child!'"

"Very well! I am her grandchild. That was not all, though—she affectionately recommended you to me, as my cousin."

"Cousin? your cousin?" repeated Claudius, without contradicting the speaker on his impression that Baboushka's face had not worn a soft expression, in his eyes.

"It would appear that you do not know yourself as Felix Clemenceau?"

"Clemenceau?" echoed the student, remembering what he had heard in the music-hall.

"Yes; your father was the famous sculptor."

Was his predilection for art a hereditary trait? the son of a celebrity? then his essays in design were unworthy of his name. Abashed, inclined to despair, having a glimpse of a tumultuous rabble shouting: "At last he is here!" before the ruddy guillotine on a raw morning, a pale, prim man between the executioner's aids, the young Clemenceau listened to the girl, who probably resembled the Lovely Iza, but looked at the dead woman at their feet.

"Yes, we are cousins! that is why I took a fancy to you at the sight. I knew this time I loved for a good reason. The band of nature—the bond of blood—connected us! But this is not the place or time to pluck leaves, and compare them, from our genealogical tree. The major has succeeded in reining in his horse, but, who cares? the old farmhouse stood a siege in the Great Napoleon's time and could mock at him now. Leave all—all these cooling pieces of carrion, and my dear grandma!" she sneered, "and let us hasten to the house where I have friends."

Like a man in a dream, Claudius, or, better, Felix Clemenceau, since this was his true title, holding the half-emptied revolver by his side, automatically allowed the strange creature to lead him from the battlefield. He was oppressed by the magnitude of the ruin he left behind: the peaceful student to whom the pencil and the eraser were alone familiar had handled firearms like "the professor" in a shooting gallery. And then the assertion—or revelation—that he was of kin not only to the old witch, who had perished in shielding him unintentionally in saving her grandchild, but to the latter. Fair as a sylph but icy-hearted as a woman of five social seasons! But the son of the guillotined wife-murderer should not be fastidious about those relatives who deigned to recognize him.

The farmhouse was a large stone and brick structure, moss-grown but firm as a castle; at its porch, three men had tranquilly awaited the result of the conflict; most of the episodes had been observed by them. Two were comfortably clothed like farmer and overseer, and showed a respectful bearing to the third. This was a man of about thirty years, but looking younger, tall, slender, elegant and proud. Not yet calm, Clemenceau vaguely recalled the refined, winning, though dissipated visage; this was the gentleman in the Harmonista who had enlightened him unawares on the antecedents of Fraulein von Vieradlers. He did not notice her companion but his stiffness disappeared as he bowed to her. Without asking for any explanation on the affray, he said to her:

"Can he—your companion—ride? The horses are under saddle. If not—"

Clemenceau replied in the affirmative to Fraulein von Vieradlers, instead of to the gentleman. He conceived an aversion to him on the spot, although his intention to include him in the pre-arranged flight was manifest. But he was the victim of circumstances and for the present he had to yield. Besides, the prospect held out was for him to continue beside the dazzling beauty, whose influence seemed more wide than her deceased ancestress.

Like many bookworms, he had entertained a humiliating opinion of the sex that makes the world move round; he was beginning to doubt, and he would retract it before long.

Kaiserina related the events briefly, while one of the farmers brought two magnificent saddle-horses round to the long, high side of the house, facing the northwest. Clemenceau mechanically mounted the bay, and the gentleman assisted the lady upon the black. Both animals were impatient to be gone, and when given the head, started off madly. This exciting pace roused the student from his lethargy, and when the steeds had settled down to a less frenzied gait, he asked what was his guide's intention.

"It is plain. You must be put across the border into France."

"France!" it seemed to him, since the revelation of his birth in that country, that the name had a charm unknown heretofore. Yes, he ought to make a pilgrimage into that sunny land where his father had been a gem in its artistic crown.

"It is your native country and you will be safer there than in Italy or Austria. Our next stage will be the little railway station to which you may see that long double silver serpent, the metal tracks, stretching across the plain."

IX

REPARATION

Fortunately for the fugitives, the poorly paid railway officials in these parts are the obsequious servants of those who liberally bribe. The station-master, though a very grand personage, indeed, in his uniform and metal-bound cap, became pliant as an East Indian waiter and accepted without question the explanation of the lady. It was she who was spokesman throughout. She said that she and her companion were play-actors and that their baggage was detained by a cruel manager of a Munich musical beer-hall; this was a wise admission as the man might have seen her at the Harmonista, or, at least, her photograph in the doorway. But they were compelled to reach Lucerne without delay or lose a profitable engagement, by the proceeds of which they could redeem their paraphernalia. While listening, the man dealt out the tickets, pocketed the gratuity which was handsomely added to a previous donation, and, without any surprise, agreed to let any one calling take away the horses; they certainly were above the means of strolling singers who had to flee from a town. Farther discussion, if he had sought it, was curtailed by the electric signal heralding the coming of a train. In eight minutes, the two were ensconced in a first-class compartment and hurried along toward the Land of Lakes.

In the sumptuous coach, the girl unburdened herself, but, with rare art or imperfect knowledge of her origin, she was more explicit on the family of her cousin than on her own. However, it was his that had made a niche in art and scandalous story.

As for Kaiserina, her mother was the eldest daughter of a Count Dobronowska, of a Polish branch of the Vieradlers, who had settled in Fuiland. The count had meddled with politics and the Czar had promptly confiscated his landed property. The loss and fear of Siberia had broken his heart. After his death, the widow passed the intervals of her grief in besieging persons of influence to obtain a restitution of the estate. Unfortunately, she had no son to fight the battle with the Czar, but two daughters were growing up with such a superabundance of charm that they promised to be no mean allies in the enterprise. But fortune did not altogether favor the widow; it is true that she interested a Russian of great wealth and political sway, but when the time came for his co-operation to be active, he played her a wicked trick. He attracted her elder daughter to him and married her. Not liking to have a mother-in-law in his mansion, he pensioned her off, with the proviso that her presence should never clash immediately with his own in any country. It is regrettable to add that Wanda, Madame Godaloff, agreed to this arrangement, and, indeed, having attained woman's goal, troubled herself not once about her parent who had schemed and plotted tirelessly for this end. The countess had brought her deer to a pretty market; but, unhappily, she gained little by the bargain compared with what she had dreamed.

She had a brother-in-law who had acted very differently from her husband. Instead of playing the patriot—and the fool—he had submitted to the tyrant and won a lucrative post at St. Petersburg. He was afraid to injure himself by giving countenance to his brother's relict, who was always seeking an audience of the Emperor. It was strongly suspected that she intended, since Wanda was out of the lists, to throw the next daughter, Iza, at the head of a Grand-duke with whom the two girls had played when all three were children at Warsaw.

The countess seemed to have educated the girl, as soon as her elder was out of the way, for a royal match. Like most Poles, Iza spoke several languages fluently, sang and played the harp and piano. She was growing lovelier than her sister because she was a purer blonde, and yet Wanda had been accounted a miracle. Remembering that, at a later period, a foreign adventuress almost inextricably ensnared one of the imperial family, the Countess Dobronowska's matrimonial project was not so insane. Some other pretender to the grand-ducal left or right hand thought it feasible, for everybody said that it was feminine jealousy that led to the countess and her "little beauty" being ordered out of the White Czar's realm. The pair, spurred on by the police of every capital, and all are in communication with St. Petersburg, at last rested in Paris. It was a favorable moment; the French government had offended the older powers by its presumption in chastising venerable Austria almost as severely as the Great Napoleon had done. The Dobronowskas were let alone in the imperial city on the Seine; but, unfortunately, the important state functionaries soon became as tired of the countess's plaints as their brothers on the Neva. Reduced to the shifts of the penniless aristocrats, the two lived like the shabby genteel. They made a desperate attempt to entrap their Grand-duke again. But the victim

ALEXANDRE DUMAS, FILS

had warning and the pair were stopped at Warsaw. Here a beam of the sun, long withheld, glanced through the clouds and transiently warmed "the marrying mamma." A distant relative of hers, one Lergins, was an attaché of the embassy and he fell in love with his "cousin" Iza, as the mother allowed the youth to call her. As he had splendid prospects and seemed to be quite another man as regarded maternal control of Wanda's husband, mamma dismissed her brilliant *ignis fatuus* and tried to have a clandestine marriage come off. But the young secretary of embassy was not of age and again she was forced to depart for Paris— that sink-hole for refugees of all sorts. His family put pressure on the officiale who in turn applied it to the luckless *intriguante*.

Farewell, the future in which a semi-imperial coronet hand gleamed! even that where a cascade of gold coin inundated the new Danae. Wearied of this constant grasping at the unattainable Iza, who had something of a heart, chose for herself, much as her elder had done, with happiness at home as the object; one fine morning, married M. Pierre Clemenceau, a young but rising sculptor. He had on the previous visit of theirs to Paris, materially befriended them. It was only gratitude after all, although he, enamored like an artist of this unrivaled beauty, would have sacrificed fortune to possess her. Indeed, he sacrificed all—even his honor, for he suffered himself to be gulled by her wiles as profoundly as he was infatuated by her charms.

At this point, as became a young woman telling of a relative's iniquity, Kaiserina glazed the facts and gave a perversion. It was later, therefore, that Felix Clemenceau learned in detail the whole mournful tale of a beautiful wanton's ingrained perfidy and a loving husband's blind confidence. The end was inevitably tragical. Lergins was decoyed by the countess to Paris, where she languished like a shark out of water. The sculptor's income did not come up to her dreams of luxury, any more than those she inspired in her daughter. She brought about a separation of the wedded pair and rejoiced when a fresh scandal necessitated a duel between the young Russian and the Frenchman. Unhappily for her revengeful ideas, it passed over harmlessly enough.

Iza remained the talk and admiration of the gay capital, although women of superior physical attractions rendezvous there. Nothing blemished her appearance; no excesses, no indulgements, not even bearing a son had a blighting effect. Unfortunately for the disseevered artist, she had been his model for the most renowned of his works and her name was inseparably intertwined with his own.

Although "crowned" as the favorite of a king who came in transparent incognito to Paris to visit her, though occupying princely quarters, outshining the fading La Mesard and the rising Julia Barucci in diamonds, Iza was still known as "the Clemenceau Statue."

Her mother, as lost to shame, was the mistress of the wardrobe in this palace; she was spiteful as a witch, and began to resemble one in her prime, bloated, red with importance and self-indulgence, before the wrinkles came many and fast. One day, annoyed at the persistency with which a friend of Clemenceau's watched the queen of the disreputable in hopes to make her flagrancy a cause for legal annulment of the marriage, she denounced him as a traitor in an anonymous letter to the fretting husband, then in Rome. Her daughter agreed to make good the assertion that the friend had failed monstrously in his trust.

Like Othello, Clemenceau swore that this demon of lasciviousness should betray no more men. The force of depravity should no farther flow to corrupt the finest and best. He entered the boudoir of the royal favorite and stabbed her to the heart. In the morning, he gave himself up to the police.

The victim was so notorious that the Clemenceau trial was a nine days' wonder. His advocate was eloquent to a fault, but that inexplicable thing, the jury, found no extenuating circumstances in the act and brought in the verdict of murder. The good men were incapable of appreciating the right he claimed to stop the blighting career of Messalina—to divorce with steel where the state of the law, then meekly following the ecclesiastical ruling, forbade any sundering of the connubial tie except by death.

He met his doom calmly and laid his head beneath the axe with a martyr's brow. Kaiserina acknowledged this.

Felix Clemenceau understood everything now. The trustees to whom he owed his subsistence-money, M. Rollinet the imperial counsel, and M. Constantin Ritz, a famous sculptor's son, and the life-companion of Clemenceau, were characters in the momentous drama which Kaiserina recited, whom he knew by correspondence.

The finger of fate, which had urged the artist to commit a homicide for morality's sake, had pointed out to his son the way which had to be followed over corpses of the young student's slaying.

Brooding over the alteration in his future, he exchanged hardly a word with his cousin, during the prolonged journey, which they continued together, as though mutual reluctance to part bound them indissolubly. Logic said there should be a powerful repugnance between those whom the shadow of the guillotine's red arm clouded. But, spite of all, Felix felt that Kaiserina was, like himself, well within the circle of infamy. Her mother was the sister of the shameful Iza, and her husband's careful guard of her proved that he doubted her walking virtuously if her unscrupulous mother stood by her side. This old Megara—who sold her offspring to worse than death—was living—seemed eternal as evil itself. It were a pious act to save Kaiserina from her as his father had tried to do with Iza. He was pleased that she seemed inclined to cling to him as though wearied of the erratic life she seemed to have led after a flight from her mother's, and which she did not describe minutely. He was also grateful that, in her allusions to his father, she did not speak with the bitterness of a blood-avenger.

They made the journey to Paris without any stoppage. He had to visit M. Ritz, for M. Rollinet was no longer there, having accepted a judgeship in Algeria. In the vehicle, carrying to a hotel where he purposed leaving her, Felix said, feelingly:

"I think I see why we were brought together. I am not to lead the life of an artist, lounging in galleries, sketching ruins and pretty girls, but one of expiation for my poor father's crime."

"Perhaps. More surely," she replied with a smile which, on her peerless lips, seemed divine, "*I* should make the faults of the Dobronowskas be forgotten."

They had arrived at the same conclusion as the journey ended, but the means had not occurred yet to either.

"Here we are," he exclaimed, as the carriage horse came to a stop.

He alighted, entered the hotel and settled for the young lady's stay. Returning, he came to help her out.

"My door will never be closed to you," she said, remembering how, in her story, her notorious ancestors had playfully suggested in a letter announcing her renunciation of her scheming mother's toils and her return to marry Clemenceau, that he might leave his door on the jar for her at all instants. "And yet, what will be the gain in our meeting again?"

"Everything for our souls, and materially! Here in France, where La Belle Iza and the executed Clemenceau point a moral, neither of us can find a mate in marriage easily. If blood stains me, shame is reflected on you. Let us efface both blood and shame by an united effort! Let our life in common force the world to look no farther than ourselves and see nothing of the disgrace beyond."

"I do not care a fig for what people think or say," said the one-night *diva*, with a curl of the lip. "And I do not understand you fully."

"Wait till I see you again, when all shall be made clear. Meanwhile, cousin—since without you I should have lost my life, or, certainly my liberty—I am eternally bound to you. It is left to you to have the bonds solemnized in the church, here, in France—my country!"

X

The Fox in the Fold

A mong the secluded villas that dot with pretty colors the suburb of Montmorency, there is none more agreeable than the Villa Reine-Claude, which was in the hands of the notary who had managed the transmission of the maintenance money to young Clemenceau. At the hint from M. Ritz, who had a debt of honor to pay the son of his dead friend, the house was rented at a nominal sum. Here Felix, as he boldly described himself by right, though the name had a tinge of mockery, installed himself with his bride. He had a portfolio of architectural sketches soon completed and, thanks to the fellowship to which his name might exercise a spell, all the old artists who had known his father, helped him manfully. Luckily, there was something markedly novel in his work.

His odd training helped him. He came from the Polish University into an unromantic society which, after its stirring up by the Great Revolution, was so levelled and amalgamated that everybody resembled his neighbor as well in manners and speech as in attire. Strong characters, heated passions, black vices, deep prejudices, grievous misfortunes, and even utterly ridiculous persons had disappeared. The country he had been reared in still thrilled with patriotism and meant something when it muttered threats to kill its tyrant—meant so much that the Czar did not pass through a Polish town until the police and military had "ensured an enthusiastic reception." But in France, tyrants and love of country were mere words to draw applause from the country cousins in a popular theatre.

Felix, though a youth, stood a head and shoulders above the level of the weaklings excluded as "finished" from these commonplace educational institutions—schools called colleges and colleges called universities, resulting necessarily from the proclamation of man's equality. He sickened at seeing the neutral-tinted lake of society, with "shallow-swells," more painful to the right-minded than an ocean in a tempest.

He soon became like the French, but not so his wife. She suffered the change of her unpronounceable name, being euphonized as "Césarine," smilingly, but life at home in a demure and tranquil suburb little suited the young meteor who had flashed across Germany. Felix saw with dismay that domestic bliss was not that which she enjoyed. For a while he hoped that she would content herself as his helpmate and the genius of the hearth when a mother.

But maternity had nothing but thorns for her. She chafed under the burden and her joy was indecent when the little boy died. Until then he had believed that the path of duty was wide enough and lined sufficiently with flowers to gratify or at least pacify her.

But Césarine was, like her aunt, a born dissolvent of society's vital elements. Ruled by a strong hand, and removed from the pernicious influence of the vicious countess, her mother had never inculcated evil to her child; on the contrary, impressed by the lesson of Iza's career, she had perhaps been too Puritanic with Césarine, whose flight from home at an early age, was like the spring of a deer through a gap in a fence. Césarine, wherever placed, sapped morality, faith, labor and the family ties.

In the new country she feared at first that she had but exchanged parental despotism for marital tyranny. But soon she perceived that nothing was changed that would affect her. On the contrary, France, in the last decade of the Empire, was more corrupt than Russia's chief towns and the dissoluteness, though not as coarse as at Munich, was more diffused. Here she was assured that she could gratify her insatiable appetite at any moment. She saw that the manners excused her; the laws guaranteed the unfaithful wife, and religion screened her; that the social atmosphere, despite slander and gossip, enveloped and preserved her; in short, it was clear that to a creature in whom wickedness developed like a plant in a hot-house, the freedom society accorded her was as delicious as that given by her husband in his trust and his devotion to art.

It seemed to her that, after the death of their first-born, his silence signified some contempt for her; in fact, she had, stupidly frank for once, expressed relief at this escape from the cares of maternity. Did he suspect that she had, not with any repugnance, precipitated its death? She feared this passionate man who, by strength of will, made himself calm, alarmed her more than an angry one would have done. Moved by instinct, for she really felt that his sacrifice to her in marrying had condoned for his father's blow at her ancestress, she tried to return him harm for good. But it is not easy for a serpent to sting a rock.

Recovered from the slight eclipse of beauty during her experience as a mother, she endeavored to make him once again her worshiper. But her tricks, her tears and her caresses seemed not to count as before when they fled from Von Sendlingen's vengeance. He remained so strictly the husband that she could perceive scarcely an atom of the lover. Then she vowed to torture him: he should no longer find a wife in her—not even a woman, still less a lovely companion; she would implant in him intolerable longing and guard that he might not gratify it—not even lull it on any side, while she would become a statue of marble to his most maddening advance. He should have no more leisure for study, but be thrilled with the incessant and implacable sensation which relaxes the muscles, pales the blood, poisons the marrow, obscures reason, weakens the will and eats away the soul.

Unfortunately for her hideous project, it was in vain that she painted the lily of her cheeks and the carmine of her lips, studied useless arts of the toilet harder than a sage muses over nature's secrets to benefit mankind, and was the peerless darling of three years ago.

He resisted her till she grew mad.

The progression of vice is such that while she believed she was simply at the degree of passion, she contemplated another crime.

She ruled the little household, for she had brought from Germany the girl Hedwig, who had been the tool of her grandmother; this silly and superstitious girl had gone once to the witch to have her fortune told and had never shaken off the bonds; these Césarine took up and drove her by them. She had led to the entrance of the girl under her roof ingeniously; Felix was cajoled into believing that she came rather on the hint of Fraulein Daniels, the Rebecca, of whom he often had agreeable and soothing memories in his distress.

Ah, she would not have interrupted his studies; she would have encouraged them; she would never have urged him to accumulate wealth to expend it in social diversions; while Césarine fretted at her splendid voice going to waste in this solitude—the house in the suburbs where no company comes.

She dreamed of holding a Liberty Hall, where her fancies might have unlicensed play and her freaks have free course. While gliding about the quiet house in a neat dress, she imagined herself in robes almost regal, with golden ornaments, diamonds and the pearls and turquoises which suited her fairness. What if the gems were set in impurities?

Alas! perfect as a husband, denying her nothing which his limited means allowed, Felix had not once an inclination to tread beside her the ballroom floor, the reception hall marbles, and the flower-strewn path at the aristocratic charity bazaar. Yet he felt firmly assured that he was destined to a great fortune. He saw the gleam of it although he could not trace the beam to its source, too dazzling. But she had no faith in him, she did not understand his value, and from the time of his certainty that they were not the unit of two hearts to which happiness accrues and where it abides, he merely resigned himself to the irremediable grief. Having vainly tried to make of her a worthy wife, and seeing that motherhood had not saved her—earthly redemption though it is of her sex—he could only watch her and prevent her resuming that orbit which would no doubt end badly, as her race offered too many examples.

On one occasion, fatigued with watching that she did not take a faulty step, he had written to Russia to see if she would find a harbor there, but the answer came from her father and sealed up that outlet. Her elopement had caused her mother fatal sorrow, and her father said plainly that he regarded her as dead. Though she came to his gates, begging her bread, he would bid his janitor drive her away. Her mother had been a good wife, but her grandmother had extorted a mint of money and, after all, nearly ruined him in the good graces of his Emperor out of spite, from her blackmail failing at last to remunerate her.

Since in Césarine, Felix found no intelligent and sympathetic companion, he took into intimacy a kind of apprentice whom he had literally picked up on the road. A slender lad of southern origin, whom a band of vagrants, making for the sea to embark to South America, had cast off to die in the ditch. Clemenceau gave him shelter, nursed him—for his wife would have nothing to do with a beggar—and to cover the hospitality and soothe the Italian's pride, paid him liberally to be his model. He was named Antonino and might have been a descendant of the Emperor from his lofty features, burning eye and fine sentiments. Healed, able to resume his journey and offered a loan to make it smooth, he effusively uttered a declaration of gratitude and devotion, and vowed to remain the slave of the man who had saved him from a miserable death.

A good work rarely goes unrewarded. Antonino, who had never touched a piece of colored chalk to a black stone, soon revealed strong gift as a draftsman and served his new master with brightness and taste.

Left lonely by his wife, each day more and more estranged, Felix loved to labor with the youth in the tasks to both congenial. That Césarine should grow jealous would be natural, but it was pique that she felt toward Felix. In Antonino, she saw the possible instrument of her vengeance. His good looks, fervid temperament, youthful impressionability, all conspired in her favor as well as the innate artistic craving which had at the first sight lifted her on a pedestal as his ideal of the woman to be idolized.

Nevertheless, the vagabond had a stronger spirit than she anticipated, and the emotion which she set down as timidity, and which protected him from the baseness of deceiving his benefactor, was due to honor. She flattered herself that she could pluck the fruit at any time, and, since this moneyless youth could not in the least appease her yearning for inordinate luxury, she cast about for another conquest.

Clemenceau would not hear of his home being turned into the pandemonium of a country-house receiving all "the society that amuses," and rigidly restricted his wife from visiting where she would meet the odd medley in the suburbs of Paris. Retired opera-singers, Bohemians who have made a fortune by chance, superseded politicians, officials who have perfected libeling into an art, and reformed female celebrities of the dancing-gardens and burlesque theatres. But, as society is constituted, it would have earned him the reputation of a tyrant if he had refused her receiving and returning the visits of the venerable Marchioness de Latour-Lagneau, to whom the Bishop always accorded an hour during his pastoral calls. This was a neighbor.

In her old Louis XIV mansion, conspicuous among the new structures, the old dame, in silvered hair which needed no powder, welcomed the "best people" in the neighborhood and a surprising number of visitors who "ran down" from the city. Considering her age, her activity in playing the hostess was remarkable. On the other hand, the "at homes" were most respectable, and the music remained "classical;" not an echo of Offenbach or Strauss; the conversation was restrained and decorous and the scandal delicately dressed to offend no ear.

Not all were old who came to the château, and the foreigners were numerous to give variety to the gatherings; but the white neck-cloth and black coat suppressed gaiety in even the rising youth, who were destined for places under government or on boards of finance and commerce.

It may be judged that an afternoon spent in such company was little change to Madame Clemenceau, and that the five o'clock tea, initiated from the English, was a kind of penitential drink. But she became a habitué, and took a very natural liking to hear again the anecdotes indicating how matters moved in Germany and Russia, where her childhood and early girlhood had passed.

One evening, she arrived late. She was exasperated: Antonino had imbibed his master's imperturbability and seemed to meet her advances with rebuking chilliness. A marked gravity governed them both of late; they shut themselves up for hours in their study, but instead of the silence becoming artists, noises of hammering and filing metal sounded, and the chimney belched black smoke of which the neighbors would have had reason to complain.

"A fresh craze!" thought Césarine, dismissing curiosity from her mind.

Dull and decorous though the marchioness' salon was, it might be an ante-chamber to a more brilliant resort beyond, while the laboratory of science leads to no place where a pretty woman cares to be.

The Marchioness had remembered her meeting with Césarine at Munich and was polite enough to express her regret that her offer of a companionship had not been accepted. "All her pets had married well," she observed, as much as to say that she would have found no difficulty in paving the lovely one with a superior to Clemenceau.

Soon Madame Clemenceau had become the favorite at the château; and, tardy as she was, the servant hastened to usher her in to her reserved chair. It was placed in the row of honor in the large, lofty drawing-room, hung with tapestry and damask curtains, and filled with funereally garbed men and powdered old dowagers. The late comer was struck by their eyes being directed with unusual interest upon a vocalist. He stood before the kind of throne on which the marchioness conceitedly installed herself.

He was singing in German, and he accompanied himself on a zither. He had an excellent baritone voice, and the ballad, simple and unfinished, became a tragic *scena* from his skill in repeating some exceptionally talented teacher's instructions.

To Césarine, the strains awakened dormant meditations; aspirations frozen in her placid home, began to melt; a curtain was gradually drawn aside to reveal a world where woman reigned over all. What she had heard from her grandmother of the magic splendor which Wanda had missed and Iza enjoyed, flashed up before her, and her heart warmed delightedly in the voluptuous intoxication of unspeakable bliss. On the wings of this melody, which, in truth, merely sought to picture the celestial dwelling of the elect, she was carried into one of those bijou palaces of the best part of the Queen City of the Universe, where the bedizened Imperia at the plate-glass window reviews an army of faultlessly-clad gentlemen filing before her, and sweetly calls out:

"This, gentlemen, is the spot where you can be amused!"

Yes, Césarine was intended to entertain men! She longed to be the central figure in the scene, however brief, of that apotheosis where Cupid is proclaimed superior to all the high interests of human conscience; this glittering stage sufficed for her, although it would have limited Felix's ideal of man's function.

In a struggle between duty and passion, she expected passion to overcome, and she concurred beforehand with this troubadour who protested that the gentler sex really held the under one in its dependence.

Radiant with pleasure and farther delighted to recognize a well-known face on the minstrel's shoulders, she hastened at the conclusion to give him her compliments. It was the young nobleman who had aided her flight with Clemenceau at Munich, and of whom she had not cherished a second thought! Better than all, while titled a baron in Germany, he held a viscount's rank in France, and his aunt, the marchioness, presented him as the last of the Terremondes.

She had not expected to meet in this coterie a gentleman who patronized the singers of a beer-hall, but the frock does not make the monk, and Baron Gratian von Linden-Hohen-Linden, Viscount de Terremonde in France, was of another species than the frequenters of Latour château.

From his income in both countries, he had the means to maintain what would have been ruinous establishments; he had the racing stud which no English peer would be ashamed of, a gallery of masterpieces acquired from living painters, an unrivaled hot-house of orchids, wolf-hounds and fox-hounds and other dogs, and the rumor went that the famous Caroline Birchoffstein, in consideration of his being a fellow-countryman, was more often seen in his box at the Grand Opera House than in her own.

The imperial court, also, not averse to being on good terms with South Germany, since Prussia was supposed to be France's greatest opponent in case Luxembourg were clutched, petted the Franco-Teuton, and regretted that he was so pleasure-loving.

To continue her thraldom over him, Césarine left not a word unsaid or a glance undelivered. In this attack, she was met halfway, for, had she been less eager, she must have seen that the viscount-baron's joy at seeing her again was sincere.

"You hesitate to ask what happened after your fortunate escape with that young student," he said, when they were allowed a few minutes together by the artful management of the hostess. "I can tell you that I had to pass through a fiery ordeal and I hope you preserved a kindly memory of one who suffered tremendously for you. Major Von Sendlingen was not an undetached person whose quarrel could be kept among private ones. On the contrary, he moved the authorities like a chess-player does the pieces, and he moved them against me. At the first, they talked of nothing less than trying me for treason, since the projected arrest of the Polish conspirator and yourself—kinswoman of the Dobronowska inscribed in the black book of the Russian and Polish police—was foiled on my territory. The major affirmed that he had seen me not only looking on at the defeat of his posse, but holding my farmers in check not to hasten to their assistance. He alleged that I had lent racehorses to you and your accomplice, for your continued flight. This Polander—"

"You can say Frenchman, now," returned Madame Clemenceau; "he is one, and my cousin. The story is long and involved and will keep to another day. It is he I married."

"Your husband!" he exclaimed, and she nodded apologetically.

"Then," sighed he, "my dream ends here—on that day when we last met."

"A learned man has said, in a lecture here, that dreams can be repeated and continued, by an effort of the will. My advice to you is to try it."

"Do not jest with me! You can see—you can be sure if you will but question—that I narrowly escaped the State's prison for helping you. Spite of all, I can love no other woman but you—"

She held up her closed fan and touched his lips with the feathery edging.

"You must not talk so—at least—here," she said, with her glance in contradiction to her words. "I am happy, or contented, strictly speaking, in my home, and as soon as my husband realizes one or two of the ideas over which he is musing, happiness must be mine. A success in art will drag him forth; he must go to Paris to be feasted in the salons and lionized in the conversaziones."

And her eyes blazed as she figured herself presiding at an assemblage of artists and patrons.

"Pardon me," said the viscount-baron. "I am afraid I add to your worry. I see that you are pining for the sphere to which your grace and charms entice you. I will do anything you order; but yet, since I, too, am an exile, and for your sake, pray do not ask me not to see you and speak of love."

"It must be thus," she replied, with half-closed eyes, turning away abruptly, as if she feared her virtuous resolution were failing. "Let our parting be forever!"

"Forever!" he repeated, following her into the window alcove, although thirty pairs of eyes regarded them. "You cannot mean that. At least, I deserve—have earned—your friendship by what I have undergone for you. Let me have a word of hope! Though divorce is not allowed in this country, death befalls any man, for while your statisticians figure out that the married live longest, they do not assert that they are immortal. Clemenceau dead, his widow may remarry. You say he is an enthusiast—one of those college-growths which run to seed without any fruit. I thought the contrary from the way he rode my horse and handled the pistols. But, being an enthusiast, how can you expect to do anything but vegetate? You will always be poor, for, if the man's ideas bore fruit, he would only sink the gains in fresh enterprises. These artists are always unthrifty, and they should wed their laundresses or their cooks. But I—though they have tied up my German revenue, and I have been practically banished—enjoy a tolerable return from my property in this Empire. I have been offered a very handsome present if I wholly transfer allegiance to the Napoleons. Would you not like to have the *entré* to the Empress's coterie and shine among the acknowledged beauties? I give you my word that your peer is not among them, and the leader would be enchanted with you. Come, suppose a little fatal accident to Monsieur—may he not suck poison off his paint brush or cut an artery with his sculptor's chisel? And, after a sojourn at Bravitz, you might return to Paris a viscountess—a countess, perhaps, and rule in a pretty court of your own!"

For a woman who had said adieu! she had lingered still listening much too long. They continued the conversation, turned into this ominous channel, in the same low key.

Césarine returned home with the sentiment of loneliness which had oppressed her almost utterly removed. She did not love Gratian, but one need not be a prisoner to understand how admirable the jailer with the outer door-key may appear. She saw in him a precious friend and ally—a worshiper who would obey a hint like a fanatic. Cautiously, at the marchioness's, and more deeply than at Munich, she made inquiries upon his pecuniary standing and was rejoiced to learn that he had not deceived her in that respect. It was left to him to be a favorite in the court, which, not succeeding in weaning away the scions of the Legitimist nobility, greeted the foreign nobles cordially and sought to attach them to its standard in foresight of a European war. One thing was certain: Gratian had illimitable resources, and the sharp-witted, who had sharp tongues, did not hesitate to aver that he was one of those spoilt children of politics who are fed from State treasuries—not such a shallow-brain as he pretended. The new type of diplomatist was like him, the Morny's, not the effete Metternich's, gentlemen who settled affairs of the State in the boudoir not in the cabinet.

Brave, gallant, dashing, craftier than his manner indicated, he was destined to play no inconsiderable part in the conflict impending; such an one might emerge from the smoke a lieutenant of an emperor and holding a large slice of territory which neither of the two contestants cared yet to rule.

Compared with a sculptor who had produced nothing—an architect whose buildings had appeared only on paper—this young noble was to be run away with, if not to be run after.

The marchioness favored their future and less public meetings, and her gardens were their scene. But while the relations of the treacherous wife with her cavalier became closer, a singular change took place in him. Instead of growing bolder, he seemed to hold aloof, and he fixed each new appointment at a longer interval. He was gloomy and absent, and she began to feel that her charm was weakening. She reproached him, and tried to find excuses for him. Everybody knew what he had lost at the races or over the baccarat-board; and she knew, according to a rhymed saying, that "lucky at love is unlucky at gambling."

"It is not that," he answered slowly, with an anxious glance around in the green avenues of trimmed trees. "I do not know why I should speak of politics to a woman; but you and I are as one: you should know the worst. I am not my own master, and they who rule me presume to dictate my course as regards my heart. Brain and sword are theirs, but I shall feel too ignoble a slave if I sacrifice my love for you to *la haute politique*."

"Sacrifice your love! That would be odious—that must not be! Do you mean that they want you to marry? How cruel!"

ALEXANDRE DUMAS, FILS

He did not smile at the absurdity of her protest, it was so sincere.

"Well, Césarine, they are blind here, and deaf to the signs along their own frontier. The French rely on a Russian alliance, when already Herr von Bismarck, the Prussian ambassador at St. Petersburg, long ago secured its suspension. Besides, the Crimean War will always be remembered against Napoleon—it is so easy not to ally oneself with England, and, considering her proverbial ingratitude, so rarely profitable. I spoke of Bismarck! This man of a million, with deep, dark eyes, fixed and unreadable, with a cold, mocking mouth, iron will and mighty brain, is soon to be pitted against Napoleon, the shadow whom you have seen. I am no soothsayer, but I can tell which must go down in the charge, and never to hold up his head again. I am one of the flies on the common wheel who will be carried into the action and smashed, whoever is the victor. I am unwilling to perish thus, when I can find in love of you a paradise on earth wherever you consent to dwell with me. Listen: I am entrusted with a prodigious sum in cash by a political organization, the headquarters of which in France are here, at the old marchioness's—a veteran puller of the wires that move the European puppets. They have practically seized my German bands, and unless I retake them at the head of a column of victorious French, I may as well say good-bye to them. As for Terremonde, the revenue is falling every quarter. If it were not for this secret service, I should be bankrupt, for the Tuileries, perhaps, suspecting my good faith, pay me only in pretty words—*a la française*. This bank which I hold tempts me sorely, Césarine, but only if you will dip into it with me. Only once in a life does a man have his great opportunity. Mine is the present. A fortune—a beauty! Never will I have such an opportunity again to found a principality in Florida or the South Seas or South America—wherever we choose to come to a rest. Speak, Césarine, are you with me? After a while, when the modern Attila has swept over France, perhaps we will like to come and view the ruins and fill our gallery with the art-treasures which the impoverished defeated ones will gladly sell."

"A large sum!" repeated the woman, frowning as her thoughts concentrated.

"Enormous! I have been changing it into sight-drafts, and we can put on our wings at a moment's notice."

"It belongs to a political organization, you say?"

"Have no qualms—it is a few drops out of a reptilian fund! No one can claim what was handed over to me without witnesses, and no receipt demanded. I make no secret: I am offering for your love the price of my honor. Only let us flee to a distance for a while. The money could not be claimed of me in a public court, but they might punish me with an assassin's bullet."

"And for me, for my happiness, you would do this? I cannot doubt you any longer, if ever I did. Enough, Gratian, I will go to the world's end with you!"

XI

A Sprat and the Whale

A few moments were enough for the two to enter the château again, where their absence had begun to arouse curiosity, though the guests were too well bred to make general remarks. With the cue that these "slow," tame gatherings were but the cloak to more important conclaves, Césarine studied them as never before. It was clear. Here and there were groups which did not waste a word on the accent of Mademoiselle Delaporte, the early history of Aimée Derclée, or the latest episode in the stage and boudoir history of "the Beauty who is also the Stupid Beast." For a certainty, conspiracy went on here at the gates of the capital; perhaps from the pretty belvedere, where the large telescope was mounted for lovers to see Venus, the sons of Mars ascertained where the batteries of siege guns should be planted to shell Parisian palaces and forts.

Two of a trade never agree, says the wisdom of our ancestors, and from that time Césarine detested Gratian. If he so easily betrayed his friends, countrymen and employers for her, what might he not do as regards her when she was older and her bloom vanished? Better not place herself under his thumb and be cast off, in some remote, barbarous region, when the caprice had worn out. But the money! What was this political league and its aims to her? For her limited education, that of a refined and expensive toy, she was ignorant of the laws and regulations governing even herself, and these laws were too subtly interwoven and inexorable for man alone to have formed them. She did not suspect the great reasons of the State in setting them in motion to accomplish collective ends and destinies, whether they wrought good or evil to individuals. Enough that they were necessary for a dynasty or a class; but in all cases, the rulers knew why they were made.

Little by little, but without loss of time, her perspicacity penetrated the disguises, although not to the motives that impelled the plotters. She centered her thoughts on the old, white-locked pianist, who silently listened to all the parties and was tolerated even when the piano was closed; he was taciturn, always blandly smiling and bent in a servile bow. Nevertheless, this was the principal of the conspirators and even the viscount-baron treated him with some deference as representing a formidable power.

One morning, Césarine came over to the marchioness's and took advantage of the drawing-room being open to be aired, to open the piano and practice an aria which she had promised at the next soirée. There was nothing but praise for her singing, and old, retired tenors and obese soprani had assured her that she had but to have one hearing in the Opera to be placed among the stars. The aged pianist had often listened to her vocalism with enraptured gaze, and she believed he, too, was her slave.

He had now glided into the room and upon the piano stool, and, as if by magic divining her wish, silently opened the piece of music for which she had been hunting. For the first time their eyes met without any medium, for he had discarded the tinted spectacles he usually wore. These were not the worn orbs of a man who had pored over crabbed partitions for sixty years. They were eyes familiar to her.

"Major Von Sendlingen!" she exclaimed, in a kind of terror; for women, being judges of duplicity, are alarmed by any one successful in disguises.

"Precisely, but do not be alarmed. You struck me in warfare, and I forgive your share in that paltry incident. I am your friend, now. By the way, as a proof of that assertion, let me tell you that the viscount is no more worthy of you than that ever-dreaming student. You think he adores you? *pfui*! only so far as you will aid the realization of his ambition. Besides, he is only an officer in our ranks; he is not unbridled, and at any moment he may be ordered away. Renounce this kind of love, my child, not durable and unendurable!"

Was this the major preaching? He who had held with the hare and run with the hounds, that is, tried to win the ascending and the declining star!

"Tell me," he continued, seriously, "tell me when you can control your heart, and it is I who will set you on that stage where you should have figured long since."

She had turned pale and she bit her lip. Her dullness in not suspecting the identity of this spy, her lover, pained her acutely. She had thought to read the Sphynx, and it had its paw upon her. Her exasperation was so keen that she determined to be revenged on both the speaker and Gratian, whose inferiority to the major was manifest.

"They shall see how *I* can plot," she thought, "and best of all, how

I carry off the prize which I need to obtain a station of my own selection in society."

One thing she saw clearly, that Von Sendlingen was out of her clutches. He still acknowledged her attractions, but he was obedient to a master more paramount. If only he had been capable of jealousy! But, no, he had alluded to the Viscount de Terremonde's flame with perfect indifference. Like Clemenceau, he would not have fought a duel for her choice. Nevertheless, her husband might have another burst of the homicidal instinct which his father showed in Paris, and he in Germany. While refusing a duel as illogical, he might fell Gratian after the model he had displayed for Major Von Sendlingen's profit in Munich.

Perhaps, though, Clemenceau was no longer jealous.

Hedwig had told her of letters addressed to Daniels which she had to mail, if Clemenceau was in correspondence with the old Jew, he would not have forgotten his daughter, the only woman of whom Césarine harbored jealousy.

But she could attain her end, profound, treacherous and bloody, like the dream of a frivolous woman going to extremes. The revelation of Von Sendlingen's presence enlightened her and filled the gap in her plan.

Meanwhile, she redoubled her efforts to entrance Gratian, and the day of their flight had but to be fixed. On hearing from Madame Clemenceau that Von Sendlingen was the chief of surveillance at the coterie, the dread that he was his rival in the contest for Césarine, filled his cup to overflowing with disgust. He had believed himself chief of the fraternity in France, and behold! another was set over him and probably reported that he neglected the business to pay court to a married woman. He felt that he was lost and that his only chance to secure the beloved one was to step outside the circle which he knew would be the vortex of a whirlpool once war was proclaimed.

"You speak most timely," he answered gravely, when she said that she was ready; "I have been notified to transfer the funds to another, in such terms as would better suit a clerk than a gentleman—a noble intelligence officer. That cursed major who learned the piano to be a means of torture to his fellow man! he has done it. He loves you no longer, and he is my enemy since I looked at him being run away with, like a raw recruit, on his first troop-horse. He will, believe me, be our destroyer unless we levant."

Nothing was easier. Since four days, Clemenceau had been invisible, even at meals. Closeted with his disciple Antonino, they worked out some more than ever preposterous conceptions into substance, in the studio where the uncompleted artistic models had been neglected. Hedwig was the false wife's bondwoman and would actively help in the removal of her trunks. The viscount had but to send a trusty man with a vehicle, and the lady could meet him at a station of the Outer Circle Railway and thence proceed to a main station for Havre or Marseilles, as they selected. The famous sight-drafts were safe on Gratian's person. With the simplicity of a child, Césarine wished again and again to gloat over them; never could she be convinced that those flimsy pieces of paper stood for large sums of ready money and that bankers would pay simply on their presentation. It was reluctantly that she restored the wallet to his inner pocket, of which she buttoned the flap, bidding him be so very, very careful of what would be their subsistence in the mango groves.

"Oh, how I love you," he said, bewildered and enthralled; "I love you because you retain, after the finished graces of woman have come, the naive traits of the guileless girl. What a joy that I divined your excellences when you were so young and that I was favored by your regard, and now am gladdened by your trustful smiles."

"I trust you so much that I could wish this money did not weigh on your bosom. I love you without it, and I shall love you as long as you live."

Seeming to be as exalted as he, she grasped both his hands and drew his face nearer and nearer hers to look him in the eyes.

"I do not ask anything of you but to be good to me. Do not reproach me for leaving my lawful lord for you! If there is a fault in quitting him who neglects me, never cast it upon me. Let us go! anywhere, if but you are ever beside me, to protect, to support and cherish!"

Her moist eyes were as eloquent as her lips, and to have doubted her, he must have doubted all evidence of his senses. And yet it was that same hand on which he had impressed a score of burning kisses that wrote these lines:

"The faithless one will take the train at Montmorency Station this night at nine."

And she deposited it, as had been agreed between her and Major Von Sendlingen in a vase on the drawing-room mantel-shelf at the marchioness's, where the viscount conducted her before their last parting. It was one of those notes which burn in the hand, and so thought the major, for he took measures, by a communication which he had established, to send it to M. Clemenceau.

Except on holidays and Sundays, when the Parisians muster in great force to promenade the still picturesque suburbs, the country roads are desolate after the return home of the clerks who have slaved at the desk in the city. One might believe oneself a hundred miles from a center of civilization.

To the station, a little above the highway level, three paths lead. On the road itself the village cart which had taken Madame Clemenceau's baggage, leisurely jogged. The lady herself, instructed by her confederate Hedwig that there was no alarm to be apprehended from the studio, strolled along a more circuitous but pleasanter way. Her husband and his pupil were, as usual, shut up in "the workshop." The studio had been changed for some new fancy of the crack-brained pair; they had packed aside the plans and models and had set up a lathe, a forge and a miniature foundry. To the clang of hammer and the squeak of file was added the detonation now and then of some explosive which did not emit the sharp sound or pungent smoke of gunpowder or the more modern substitutes' characteristic fumes.

At each shock, Césarine had trembled like the guilty. They had told her that she was born in St. Petersburg when her mother was startled by the blowing up of the street in front of their house by an infernal machine intended to obliterate the Czar; in the sledge in which he was supposed to be riding, a colonel of the *chevalier-gardes*, who resembled him, had been injured, but the incident was kept hushed up.

One of the old servants whose age entitled his maunderings to respect among his superstitious fellows had, thereupon, prophesied that the new-born babe would end its life by violence.

"It is time I should quit the house," she muttered, drawing her veil over her eyes, of which the lids nervously trembled. "I cannot hear those pop-guns without consternation."

She hurried forth without a regret, and passed, as a hundred times before, the family vault in the cemetery, where her murdered infant reposed, without a farewell glance, although she might never see the place again.

On coming within sight of the station, she perceived a solitary figure, that of a man, in a fashionable caped cloak, crossing the fields in the same direction as hers. It was probably the viscount going to it separately in order not to compromise her and give a clue to the true cause of her flight.

Sometimes the unexpected comes to the help of the wicked. Incredible as it appeared, she received, on the eve of her departure, a telegram from Paris. At first she thought it a device of Viscount Gratian's to cover her elopement, but it was not possible for him to have imagined the appeal. It was from her uncle, who, traveling in France, and intending to pay her a visit since she was married honorably, was stricken with a malady. He awaited her at a hotel. Even Von Sendlingen could not have drawn up this message too simple not to be genuine and too precise in the genealogical allusions not to be a Russian's and a Dobronowska's.

She regarded this cloak as the act of her "fate"—the evil person's providence. She handed the paper to Hedwig to be given to her husband as an explanation at a later hour.

Césarine was still watching him when she saw him disappear suddenly. It was in crossing an unnailed plank thrown across a drain-cutting. This must have turned or broken under his feet unexpectedly, for his fall was complete. In the ditch which received him, darkness ruled but it seemed to Césarine that more shadows than one were engaged in deadly strife, standing deep in the mire. They wore the aspect of the demons dragging down a soul in an infernal bog.

What increased the horror was the silence in which the tragedy was enacted; probably the unfortunate Gratian had been seized by the throat as soon as he dropped confused into the assassin's clutches.

Halfway between this scene and the dismayed looker on, another shadow rose and appeared to take the direction to accost her instead of hurrying to the victim's succor. This made him resemble an accomplice, and, breaking the spell, Césarine hurried on without the power to force a scream for help from her choking throat.

At that moment, while a strong fascination kept her head turned toward the field, a long beam from the locomotive's head-light shot across it. It fell for an instant on the solitary form and though its arm made an upward movement to obscure its face, she believed that she recognized her husband.

Clemenceau on her track! Clemenceau, in concord with the bravest who had smothered her gallant in the mud! she had scorned him too much! He was capable even of cowardly acts, of being revenged for this renewed disgrace upon his ill-fated house!

This time her feet were unchained and she flew up the hill. She thought of nothing but to escape the double revenge of the husband she wronged, and Von Sendlingen whom she had cheated.

She took her ticket mechanically and entered a coach marked for "Ladies Only."

They whisked toward Paris swiftly, before any sinister face looked in at the window, or she had time to reflect. In her pocket was the real case of the sight-drafts for which she had palmed a duplicate filled with cut paper, upon the unlucky viscount. She was rich enough to make a home wherever money reigns—a broad enough domain.

The arrival of her relative and the summons to his sick-bed made her pause in her movements suddenly altered by the death of the viscount. She was almost happy in her foresight by which she had defrauded him and his associates. Now, the loss of him stood by itself; she was free to use the money as she pleased. She feared Von Sendlingen but little, since she would have a good start of him if he pursued.

Should she keep on or see her uncle? Pity for him, a stranger, perhaps dying in a hotel, most inhospitable shelter to an invalid, did not enter her heart. She had seen her lover murdered without a spark of communication, and was now glad that he could never call her to account for the theft. But a vague expectation of benefiting by the pretense of affection—the desire to have some support in case of Von Sendlingen attacking—the excuse and cover her ministration at the sick-bed would afford, all these reasons united to guide her to the Hotel de l'Aigle aux deux Becs, in the rue Caumartin.

Her uncle was no longer there. His stroke of paralysis had frightened the proprietor who suggested his removal to a private hospital, but M. Dobronowska had preferred to be attended to in the house, a little out of St. Denis, of an acquaintance. It was Mr. Lesperon's, the abode of a once noted poetess, whose husband had enjoyed Dobronowska's hospitality in Finland and who had tried to repay the obligation.

Césarine recalled the name; this lady had been a friend of her aunt's and she felt she would not be intruding. After playing the nurse, by which means she could ascertain whether she would be remembered generously in the patient's will, she could continue her flight or retrace her steps.

Under cover of Hedwig, she could learn, secretly if she preferred it, all that occurred at Montmorency. She found her grand-uncle broken with age and serious attack; he was delighted by her beauty and to hear that she was so happy in her married life! Evidently he was rich, and she had not acted foolishly in going to see him.

Madame Lesperon and her husband recalled her grandmother—whose death she did not describe—and her aunt, over whose fate they politely blurred the rather lurid tints. Madame Lesperon, as became a poetess, saw the loveliness of Clemenceau's idea of separation in marrying his cousin and expressed a wish to compliment him face-to-face. Césarine was not so sure that he would come to town to escort her home, he was so engrossed in an important project.

She let three days pass without writing a line, alleging that she had not the heart while her dear uncle was in danger and that her husband knew, of course, where she was piously engaged.

The next morning, Madame Lesperon, a regular reader of the newspapers in expectation of the announcement of her poems having at last been commended by the Académie, came up to the sick-room with the *Debats*.

"Ah, sly puss," said she, with a smile, "let me congratulate you. One can know now why you were so close about your husband's mysterious project. Rejoice, dear, for all France rejoices with you."

Césarine stared all her wonder. The newspapers trumpeting her husband's name and not in the satirical tone in which the people hail a disaster to a George Dandin.

"The privately appointed committee which has been for some weeks thoroughly investigating the marvelous invention—a revolution in truth—in gunnery, at the Villa Reine-Claude, Montmorency, have deposited a preliminary report at the Ministry of War. We are not at liberty to state more than the prodigious result. On a miniature scale, but which could be enlarged from millimètres to miles without, we are assured, affecting the demonstration, it has been proved that the new gun will throw solid shot twelve miles and its special shell nearly fifteen. The model target was a row of pegs representing piles strongly driven into clay, a little apart, with the interstices filled with racks of stones. Two of the new-shaped projectiles dropped on this mark, left not enough wood to make a match and enough stone to strike a light upon it, while not a splinter of the missile could be found. Judge what would happen if they had fallen on a regiment or into a city. Thanks to the unremitting devotion of this son of France, his country can regard with complacency the monstrous preparations for unprovoked war which a rival realm is ostentatiously making."

The other journals repeated the paragraph in much the same language. The evening edition added that the happy inventor would not have to wait long for his reward. The Emperor, always a connoisseur in artillery, had sent him ten thousand francs from his private purse simply as a faint token of appreciation. "Those familiar with what, in these rapid times, is the ancient history of Paris, may remember that a stain was attached to the name of Clemenceau. In his son, it will shine untarnished, and go down to posterity glorious with lustre."

"What a fool I have been," thought Césarine. "I fled with a silly fellow who had no more sense than to fall into a trap, for a paltry handful of drafts that may not be paid on presentation, and desert a husband who will be one of the millionaire-inventors of his country!"

Reflecting in the night, she radically reversed her programme.

Her uncle had recovered from the stroke but the physician warned him that the next would kill him. He was happy in the cares of the Lesperons and his grandniece, none of whom would be forgotten when the hour struck for him to leave his worldly goods. Césarine could quit him in confidence of a handsome inheritance at not a distant day.

Her flight and absence were commendable in the world's most censorious eyes. Only one thought perplexed her: was it her husband who had officiated at the execution of her gallant? If so, her lie would not hold. But in doubt a shameless sinner chooses to brazen it out.

"I should be a confirmed imbecile to let this chance go and not resume my authorized position. Ah, his time, without infamy, I can preside at the board where the high officials will gladly sit—I shall have generals at my feet, perhaps a marshal! Yes, I will go home and brazen it out!"

XII

When the Cat's Away

Ten days after the sudden departure of Madame Clemenceau from her residence, a little before daybreak, Hedwig came down through the house to draw up the blinds and open the windows. She carried a small night-lamp and was not more than half awake.

It was the noise of the great invention which had turned the tranquil group of villas and cherry orchards into a rendezvous for the singular admixture of artilleries and scientific luminaries. The peaceful villa entertained a selection of them nightly and it is astonishing how heartily the military men ate and the professors drank, for the enthusiasm had turned all heads.

Hedwig entered the fine old drawing-room where the symposium had been held. It was a capacious room, not unlike an English baronial hall, the doorways and windows were furnished with old Gobelin tapestry and the heavy furniture was of mahogany, imported when France drew generously on her colonies. The long table had been roughly cleared after supper by the summary process of bundling all the plates up in the cloth. On it had been replaced, for the final debate, drawings and models of the guns considered absolute after the novel Clemenceau Cannon. On a pedestal-pillar stood a large clock, representing, with figures at the base, the forge of Vulcan; his Cyclops had hammered off six strokes a little preceding the servant's entrance.

"A quarter past six," she said, yawning. "It will soon be light."

She drew the curtains and pulled the cord which caused the shade to roll itself up in each of the three tall windows, before returning to the table where she had left her now useless lamp. With a half-terrified look, she began to arrange the pretty little cannon, exquisitely modeled in nickel and bronze, and miniature shot, shell, chain-shot, etc., which she handled with a curiosity rather instinctive than studied. In the midst of her mechanically executed work, she was startled by a gentle rapping on the plate-glass of a window. The sight of a face in the grey morning glimmer startled her still more, but, luckily, she recognized it. After hesitation, she crossed the room in surprise and unbolted the two sashes, which opened like double doors.

"Hedwig!" said a woman's voice warily speaking, "open to me!"

The girl held the sashes widely apart, muttering:

"The mistress! why the mischief has she come back when we were getting on so nicely."

But, letting the new-comer pass her, she tried to smoothe her face, and don the smile as stereotyped in servants as in ballet-dancers, while she continued the letting in of the daylight to gain time to recover her countenance.

Césarine threw off a cloak, trimmed with fur, and more suitable for a colder season, but it was a sable with a sprinkling of isolated white hairs most peculiar and a present from her granduncle. She tottered and seemed weak, for she had concluded that an affection of illness would aid her re-entrance. As Hedwig extinguished the lamp, she sank into an arm-chair. She curiously glanced around and inhaled with a questioning flutter of the nostrils the lasting odor of cigars and Burgundy, which the air retained. In this gloomy apartment where she had often sat alone, sure not to be disturbed, the suggestion of uproarious jollity hurt her dignity. A singular way to express sorrow and shame at the loss of a wife by calling in boon companions! This did not seem like Felix Clemenceau, sober and austere, thus to drown care in champagne.

"Are you alone, girl?" she inquired, looking round with a powerful impression that the house had unexpected inmates.

"Yes. No one is up yet in the house," responded Hedwig, sharing her mistress' uneasiness, though from a less indefinite reason; "at all events, nobody has come down yet. But how did you see that it was I who came in here before the shades were drawn up?"

"Well, I had made a little peep-hole to see what my husband and his fellow conspirator were about, in the time before they shut themselves up in their studio. But, if it is my turn to put questions," she went on with some offended dignity, "how is it that the back door is bolted as well as barred and that I have had to sneak in like a malefactor?"

"If you please, madame, it is the rule to be very careful about fastening up, since you went away."

"Oh, on the principle of locking the stable-door when the steed—"

"Oh! they fear the loss of something which, without offense, I may say, they esteem more highly than you."

Hedwig answered without even a little impertinence and the other did not resent what sounded discourteous.

"Then they do not lock up to keep me out?" she questioned.

"It might be a little bit that way, too."

"It is a new habit. Did the master suggest it?"

"Not the master altogether, madame, but his partner."

"Eh! do you mean Antonino? Monsieur had already lifted him up to be his associate, his confidant, his friend, to the exclusion of his lawful friend and confidant, his wife—and now, does he make him his partner?"

"No, madame; though he has a good fat share in the enterprise. It is M. Daniels who found the funds for the new company in which the master is engaged, and he manages the house to leave the master all his time to go on inventing and entertaining the grand folks we have to dinner."

"Mr. Daniels! not the old Jew who played that queer straight trumpet at Munich—"

"Yes, the turkophone! Ah, he has no need to go about the music halls now—he is, if not rich, the man who leads rich men by the nose, to come and deposit their superfluous cash in our strong-box."

And she pointed fondly to a large iron-clamped coffin which occupied the space between two of the windows. It was a novelty, for Césarine did not recollect seeing it before. Continuing her survey, it seemed to her that she noticed a different arrangement of the ornaments than when she was queen here, and that the fresh flowers in the vases and two palmettoes in urns were placed with a taste the German maid had never shown.

"Let me see! this Jewish Orpheus had a daughter—"

"Exactly; she never leaves him. She has rooms within his just the same as at our house in Munich. It appears that Jew parents trust their pretty daughters no farther than they can see them. But I do not blame M. Daniels," went on Hedwig, enthusiastically, "she is so lovely!"

Césarine rose partly, supporting herself with her hands on the arms of the chair. Her eyes flashed like blue steel and her whole frame vibrated with kindled rage.

"Do you mean to tell me, girl, that Mademoiselle Rebecca—as her name went, I think—is now the mistress of my house?"

"In your absence," returned Hedwig, drawlingly, "somebody had to preside, for neither the master, the old gentleman nor M. Antonino take the head of the dinner-table with the best grace. It is true that our guests are not very particular if the wine flows freely. I do not think the young lady likes the position, for I know the old, be-spectacled professors are as pestering with their attentions as the insolent officers. She would have been so delighted at the relief promised by your return that she would run to meet you and you would not have been repulsed at the door."

"I daresay," replied Madame Clemenceau, frowning, and tapping the waxed wood floor impatiently with her foot. "I did not care to announce my return home with a flourish of trumpets. I was not averse to taking the house by surprise, and seeing what a transformation has gone on since I went away. Besides, it is desirable, not to say necessary, that I should speak with you before seeing the others."

Hedwig pouted a little.

"You ought to have written to me, madame, as we were agreed, I thought; I have been on tenterhooks because of your silence. I did not even guess where you were."

"I did not wish it known for a while, and even then, it appears, I spoke too soon," said Césarine gloomily.

"You did not want me to know, madame?" questioned the servant in surprise and with a trace of suspicion.

"Not even you," and hanging her head, she sank into meditation, not pleasant, to judge by her hopeless expression.

The servant, who had the phlegmatic brain of her people, was stupefied for a little time, then, recovering some vivacity, she inquired hesitatingly as though she was never at her ease with the subtle woman.

"Is madame going away without more than a glance around?"

"Why do you talk such nonsense?" queried her mistress, looking up abruptly.

The girl intimated that the mysterious entrance portended secrecy to be preserved. And, again, the lady had come without baggage, even so much as in eloping from home. But Madame Clemenceau explained, with the most natural air in the world, that she had walked over from the railway station, where her impedimenta remained.

"Walked half a mile?" exclaimed Hedwig, who knew that the speaker had been vigorous enough at Munich, but, since her marriage, and living at Montmorency, she had assumed the popular air of a semi-invalid, "So you are strong in health again?"

"Yes; but I have been very unwell," replied the lady, sinking back in the chair as she remembered the course she had intended to adopt. "I was very nearly at death's door," she sighed. "I really believed that I should nevermore see any of you, my poor husband and you others. Do you think that anything hut a severe ailment could excuse me for my strange silence—my apparently wicked absence?"

Hedwig went on going through the form of dusting the huge metal-bound chest, which had attracted the mistress' eyes as a new article of furniture. Had her husband turned miser since Fortune had whirled on her wheel at his door as soon as she quitted it? It was not Hedwig's place, and it was not in her power to solve enigmas, so she answered nothing.

"My uncle was terribly afflicted," said the lady.

"Your uncle?"

Hedwig's incredulous tone implied that she had not believed in the authenticity of the telegram.

"Yes; my granduncle. He was within an ace of dying, and the shock made me so bad, after nursing him toward recovery, it was I who stood in peril of death. My friends sent for a priest and I confessed."

The girl opened her eyes in wonder and a kind of derision, for she did not belong to the aristocratic creed.

"Confessed?" reiterated she; "ah, yes; people confess when they are very bad. Was it a complete confession, madame?" she saucily inquired.

"Complete as all believers should make when on the brink of the grave," replied Madame Clemenceau, in her gravest tone to repress the tendency to frivolity, for she had not resented the incredulity as regarded herself.

"I dare say," said Hedwig, who certainly had one of her lucid intervals, "it is as when a body is traveling, one is in such a hurry that something is forgotten. You went away so sharply that you forgot to say good-bye to the master! if you spoke at all! Whatever did the father-confessor say?"

"He gave me very good advice."

"Which you are following, madame?"

"When one not only has seen death smite another beside one but flit close by oneself, I assure you, girl, it forces one to reflect. Oh, how dreadful the nights are in the sick chamber, with a night-light dimly burning and the sufferer moaning and tossing! Then my turn came to occupy the patient's position, and it was frightful. Can you not see I am much altered—horrid, in fact?"

Hedwig shook her head; without flattery, well as her mistress assumed the air of languor, her figure had not been affected by any event since the slaying of the Viscount Gratian, and her countenance was unmarred by any change except a trifling pallor.

"Yes; after my uncle grew better, I was indisposed and should have died but for the cares of an old friend, Madame Lesperon the Female Bard. But you would not know this favorite of the Muses. You are not poetically inclined, Hedwig!" she added, laughingly. Rising with animation, "but that makes no matter! I am glad to see you home again. I thought of you, Hedwig, and I have bought you something pretty to wear on your days out—bought it in Paris, too."

"Is that so?" exclaimed the girl, much less absent and saucy in the curl of her lip; "you are always kind."

"Yes; they are in my new trunk, for which you had better send the gardener at once. He is not forgotten either. There is a set of jewelry, too, in the old Teutonic style. They say now in Paris that any idea of war between France and Prussia is absurd, and there is a revulsion in feeling—the vogue is all for German things. I am not sorry that I know how to dress in their style, and I have some genuine Rhenish jewelry, which become me very well."

"I see that madame has indeed not altered," remarked Hedwig, plentifully adorned with smiles, as the sunshine streamed into the grave apartment. "You have fresh projects of captivating the men!" Césarine smiled also, and nodded several times.

"Here?" cried the girl, in surprise.

"Certainly here, since I understand you are receiving company in shoals."

"That is all over now, madame, and I am sorry, for the callers were very generous to me. It appears that the War Ministry do not approve of strangers running about Montmorency and into the abode of the great inventor of ordinances—"

"Ordnance, child," corrected Madame Clemenceau.

"And the house is sealed up, as you found it, against all comers. We have nobody here for you to try graces upon except Mademoiselle Rebecca's papa—and he being a Jew, you must not go near him, fresh from the confessional."

Madame Clemenceau seemed to be musing.

"I forgot—there's young M. Antonino," continued the servant.

Césarine made a contemptuous gesture, expressive of the conquest being too easy.

"Such sallow youth are best left to platonic love, it's more proper, and to them, quite as entertaining."

"Well, madame," said Hedwig, like a cheap Jack, holding up the last of his stock, "they are the only men I can offer you; for, since we have been firing off guns and cannon, our neighbors have moved away right and left—we are so lonely. No servant would stay a week!"

"Those the only men?" said the returned fugitive; "Hedwig, this is not polite for your master."

"Oh, madame, a husband never counts."

"You are very much mistaken. He does *count*—his money, I suppose, if that is his cash-box." And, yielding to her girlish curiosity, she went over to the steel-plated chest and avariciously contemplated it,

"Not at all, madame. That is where they lock up the writings and drawings about the new gun!"

"Oh, what do they say?"

"Nothing a Christian can make head or tail of," returned the servant reservedly. "They write now in a hand no honest folk ever used. An old man who ought to have known better—the Jew—he taught the master, and they call it siphon—"

"Cipher, I suppose? It appears the newspapers are right!" resumed the lady. "He is a great man!" and she clapped her hands.

Hedwig regarded her puzzled, till her brow unwrinkling at last, she exclaimed:

"Upon my word, I believe you have fallen in love with master."

"You might have said: I am still in love. That is why I return to his side."

"If you tell him that is the reason," said this speaker, who used much Teutonic frankness to her superiors, "you will astonish him more than you did me by popping in this morning. He will not believe you."

Madame Clemenceau smiled as those women do who can warp men round to their way of thinking.

"But he will! Besides, if it is a difficult task, so much the better—when a deed is impossible, it tempts one."

"Well, as far as I can see, madame, that is an odd idea for you to have had when far away from master."

"Pish! did you never hear the saying that 'Absence makes the heart grow fonder?' Oh, girl, I had so much deep meditation as I stared at the dim night-light," and she shuddered and looked a little pale.

"Well, madame, I should have rolled over and shut my eyes," said the matter-of-fact maid.

There was more truth in the lady's speech than her hearer gave her credit for. She was no exception to the rule that the wives of great inventors almost never properly appreciate them. By the light of his success, breaking forth like the sun, she feared that the greatest error of her life had been made when she miscomprehended him. In her dreams as well as her insomnia, it was Clemenceau that she beheld, and not the gallants who had flashed across her uneven path, not even the viscount, whose spoil was her nest-egg. Alas! it was a mere atom to the solid ingot which her misunderstood husband's genius had ensured. She had perhaps lost the substance in snapping at the shadow.

"Any way, I love my husband," she proceeded, moaning aloud, and resting her chin in the hollow of her hand—the elbow on the table, to which she had returned and where she was seated. "I am sure now."

"No doubt," said the servant, unconsciously holding the feather duster as a soldier holds his rifle; "madame has heard about our great discoveries in artillery? They are revo—revolutionizing—oof! What a mouthful—the military world!"

"Yes; I read the newspaper accounts during my convalescence," replied Madame Clemenceau.

"Then you fell in love with your husband because of his cannon," said Hedwig, laughing. "I do not see what connection there is between them, and, in fact," reflecting a little and suddenly laughing more loudly, "I hear that cannons produce breaches rather than re-union. Well, after all, if cannons do not further love, its a friend to glory and riches! The Emperor, some of our visitors said, is very fond of artillery, and he will give master immense contracts from the report of the examining committee being so favorable."

"Really, Hedwig, you are becoming quite learned from the association with scientists. What long words you use!

"That's nothing," said the servant, complacently.

"There is no word difficult in French to a German. but I can tell you that, as we cannot live on air, and these promises do not bear present fruit, master has been forced to sell this house."

"Eh! why is that? I like the place well enough."

"You were not here to be consulted, madame, and, we wanted the money. Master does not wish to be obliged to M. Daniels and, besides, he, too, does not get in the cash for his company any too rapidly. Master ran into debt while making his guns and cannon, and we have been pinched for ready money."

"I am glad to hear it!" exclaimed Césarine, without spitefulness, and with more sincerity than she had spoken previously.

The girl stared without understanding.

"I have money—cash—to help him, and it will be far more proper for him to be obliged to his wife than to strangers. Besides, I should not tax him with usurious interest," she said maliciously.

"Money, madame," said the servant with her widely opened eyes still more distending.

"I have two hundred thousand francs, that is, nearly as many marks, coming from my good uncle who is a little late in doing me a kindness—but my attention touched him. But do I not hear steps—somebody at last moving in the house?"

"Very likely," replied the servant tranquilly, "but nobody will come in here, before master has breakfast. Since he stores his secrets in that chest, and no company drops in, this is a hermitage. Mademoiselle Rebecca is not one of the prying sort."

Madame Clemenceau, who had risen with more nervous anxiety than she cared to display to the servants, stood by her chair, looking toward the door.

"Has he talked about me, sometimes?"

"Master? never—not before me, anyway, madame."

"Yet you gave him the telegram that explained all?"

"Yes, madame; but not until some time after your departure and when master had returned from a promenade alone. I know he was alone, because M. Antonino was racing about to show him some of his wonderful experiments."

Beyond a doubt, it was Clemenceau who had stood witness to the tragedy in the meadow. Hence his inattention to the Russian's despatch, which he naturally would disbelieve, and probably to her prolonged absence.

It was humiliating that he had not searched for her.

"What! no allusion to my stay—no hint of my possible return?"

"His silence has been perfect as the grave. Next morning after you left and did not return, master looked at the cover which I had from habit placed for you, and remarked: 'Oh, by the way, you will have another to lay to-morrow, as we shall have two guests for, I hope, a long time.' He meant the Danielses, madame. Their coming made it a little livelier for him and M. Antonino."

"It looks like a plot," murmured Césarine, indignantly, as she pictured the happy reunions out of which she had been displaced in memory—not even her untouched plate left as memento! her chair taken by Rebecca Daniels!

"Mr. Daniels is like M. Antonino, too!" continued Hedwig. "Not only is he getting up the company for the master's inventions, but for the young gentleman's—he has made such a marvel of a rifle— they put a tin box into it, and lo! you can fire three hundred shots as quick as a wink! I walk in terror since I heard of it! and I touch things as if they would go off and make mince-meat of me in the desert to it."

"Never mind that!" cried Madame Clemenceau, testily.

"Although the connection between piping at music halls and enchanting the bulls and bears of the Bourse is not clear to me, I can understand how M. Daniels, as a financial agent, should be lodging under our roof, but his daughter—"

"She is our housekeeper, and, to tell the plain truth, madame, we have lived nicely, although money was scarce, since she ruled the roost. Ah, these Jews are clever managers!"

Césarine did not like the earnest tone of praise and hastened to say bluntly:

"I suppose, then, she threw the spell over him again which once before, at Munich, caused him, a tame bookworm, to fight for her like a king-maker?"

"Mademoiselle Rebecca! she act the fascinatress!" exclaimed Hedwig, with a burst of indignation.

"What is there extraordinary, pray, in a husband, apparently deserted by his wife, paying attention to another handsome young woman?"

"Why, madame, you must forget that master is the most honorable gentleman as ever was, and that Mademoiselle Rebecca is a perfect lady!" Then, perceiving that her enthusiasm on the latter head was not welcome to the hearer, Hedwig, added: "but it does not matter. We are receiving no more company, lest the great secret leak out, and so we don't need a lady at the table. She is going away with her father, who is to open the Rifle Company's offices in Paris, and that's all!"

"It is quite enough!" remarked the other, frowning.

"What is the last word about him?" inquired the servant, "the viscount-baron, I mean."

"M. de Terremonde?"

"Yes; you haven't said a word about him."

"Do you not know?" began Césarine, shuddering as the scene in the twilight arose before her on the background of the sombre side of the room.

"He was not likely to return hereabouts. Master might have tried the new rifle upon him," with a suppressed laugh.

"Well, if you do not know, I need only say that I am perfectly ignorant of his whereabouts. I went to town without his escort, and I suppose— if he has disappeared," she concluded with emphasis, "that he has gone on a journey of pleasure, or is dead."

"Dead," uttered Hedwig, shuddering in her turn, "in what a singular tone you say that word."

"What concern is it of mine?" questioned Madame Clemenceau, pursing up her lips to conceal a little fluttering from the dread she felt at the effectual way in which her lover had been removed from mortal knowledge. "I do not mind declaring that, if I am given any choice in the matter, I should prefer his taking the latter course."

Hedwig's teeth chattered so that the other looked hard at her till she faltered the explanation:

"Your way of saying things, madame, gives me cold shivers up and down the back—ugh! Why, that gentleman was over head and ears in love with you!"

"That is why he probably went under so quickly, and could not keep his head above water!"

"I thought you liked him a goodish bit—"

"I—oh!"

An explosion, very sharp and peculiarly splitting the air, resounded under the windows and caused Césarine to clap her hands to her ears in terror.

XIII

The Revolution in Artillery

O
h, what is that?" muttered Césarine, with white lips.

Hedwig laughed, but going to the window, calmly replied:

"It is only the master—no, it is M. Antonino, who is trying the rifle they invented. Isn't it funny, though—it does not use powder or anything of that sort—it does not shoot out fire, but only the bullet, and there's no smoke! I never heard of such a thing, and I call it magic!"

"A gun without powder, and no fire or smoke," repeated Madame Clemenceau. "It is, indeed, a marvel!" and she approached the window in uncontrollable curiosity. "Is he going to shoot again?"

"Well, he gets an appetite by popping at the sparrows before breakfast. He is not much of a marksman like master, who is dead on the center, every military officer says—but, in the morning, the birds' wings are heavy with dew, and he makes a very pretty bag now and then. What must the sparrows think to be killed and not smell any powder!"

"I wish you would tell him to go farther, or leave off!" said Césarine, looking out at the young man with the light rifle, fascinated but fearing.

"The obedience will be more prompt if you would tell him, madame," returned the maid, "for M. Antonino would do anything for you. To think that there should really be something that frightens you!"

"After my illness, I am afraid of everything."

"Very well, I will stop him."

Opening the window, Hedwig called to the Italian by name, and said, on receiving his answer:

"Please not to shoot any more!"

"Why not?" came the reply in the mellow voice of the Italian.

"Come in and you'll learn." But she shut the window to intimate that he was to enter the house by the door as he had issued, and hastily returned to her mistress.

The latter had tottered to the side-board, and seized a decanter, but, in the act of pouring out a glass of water, she paused suspiciously.

"Is this good to drink?" she warily inquired.

"Of course, though you are quite right—they do juggle with a lot of queer acids and the like dangerous stuff here! They give me the warning sometimes after their *swim-posiums*, as they call the sociables, not to touch anything till they come down, for poisons are about. Ugh! But do not drink so much cold water so early in the morning—it is unhealthy. If it were only good beer, now, it would not matter! *Ach*, Müchen!" and Hedwig vulgarly smacked her lips.

"After my illness I have been always thirsty, and, sometimes, I seem to have infernal fires in my bosom!" sighed Madame Clemenceau, putting down the glass with a hand so hot that the crystal was clouded with steam.

Her teeth chattered, as a sudden chill followed the flush, and Hedwig shrank back in alarm—the beautiful face became transformed into such a close likeness to a wolf's. "You need not be scared any more, for he has come into the house. Here he is, too!" and she sprang to the door, as well to open it to M. Antonino, as to screen her mistress until she cared to reveal her presence.

Perhaps it was application to the work and not pining over the absence of Césarine, but the Italian showed evidence of sleeplessness and his pallor had the unpleasant cast of the Southerners when out of spirits.

His eyes were enfevered and his lips dry and cracked. He carried a handsome fowling-piece, which presented, at first glance, no feature of dissimilarity to the usual pattern except that trigger and hammer were absent, and the rim of the barrel was not blackened from the recent discharge.

"What did you stop me for when I had hardly more than begun my sport and practice?" he inquired.

"Put down that devil's own gun, sir monsieur," said Hedwig, "if you please."

"Why, what's the matter?" said he, while obeying by standing the rifle in a corner. "I thought you Germans were all daughters or sweethearts of soldiers."

"Ay, and most of us women would make as good soldiers as they have here; but I was speaking because you gave a shock to madame."

Stepping aside, Antonino discovered Madame Clemenceau, who smiled softly.

"Oh, madame!" exclaimed Antonino, at the height of astonishment, not unmixed with gladness. "I beg your pardon; I am very sorry—I mean glad—that is, I was not aware—if I had had any idea you were home—"

"You could not have known," she answered in a gentle voice. "I was too eager to get back, to delay to send a line. As for the noise, another time it might not matter, but I came here by an early morning train and I had no rest before I started. I am very fatigued and nervous, and the shot so sudden, surprised me. For a little while to come, I should like you to repeat your experiments with firearms at a distance from the house. Is—is that the new kind of rifle?" she inquired, with the timidity of a child introduced to the new watchdog.

"Yes, madame!" and his eyes blazing with pride, he proceeded, as he crossed the room and returned with the firearm, "it is altogether a new invention. Master is an innovator, indeed!"

"Do you object to showing it to me?" continued Césarine, pleased that the enthusiasm gave an excuse for her not entering into an explanation of her absence which, even if more plausible than that Hedwig had doubtingly received, would require all of Antonino's affectionate faith in her to win credence. "I do not object. Even those experienced in the old weapons can inspect it and not learn much," he went on, with the same pride; "but I thought it frightened you!"

"It did—it does, but I ought to overcome such a ridiculous feeling! I, above all women, being a gun-inventor's wife! Is it loaded?" she asked, while hesitatingly holding out her hand to take it.

Hedwig had prudently backed over to the window which she held a little open to make a leap out for escape in case of accident. Her mistress took the rifle and turned it over and over; certainly, it resembled no gun she had ever handled before. Its simplicity daunted her and irritated her.

"It seems to have two barrels," she remarked, "although one is closed as if not to be used. Is it double-barrelled?"

"There are two barrels, or, more accurately speaking, a barrel for discharge of the projectile and a chamber for the explosive substance, which is the secret."

"Then you load by the muzzle, like the old-fashioned guns?"

"Oh, no; there is no load, no cartridge, as you understand it; only the missiles, and they are inserted by the quantity in the breach."

"And there is no trigger or hammer!" exclaimed Césarine, not yet at the end of her wonder.

"Obsolete contrivances, always catching in the clothes or in the brambles, and causing the death or maiming of many an excellent man. We have changed all that by doing away with appendages altogether.

This disc, when pressed, allows so much of the explosive matter to enter the barrel and it expels the missile by repeated expansions."

"How very, very curious!" exclaimed Madame Clemenceau, returning the piece to Antonino with the vexed air of one reluctantly giving up a puzzle to the solution of which a prize was attached. "I should like you to make it clear to me—"

"The government forbids!" said the Italian, smiling, and assuming a look of preternatural solemnity to make the lady smile and Hedwig laugh respectfully. "And, then, the company we are getting up, lays a farther prohibition on us. However, you are in the arcana—you are one of the privileged, I suppose, and if M. Clemenceau does not expressly bar my lessons, you shall learn how to knock over sparrows for your cat."

"You will instruct me?"

"Most gladly!"

"That is nice of you, and I am so sorry at having interrupted your experiments."

"Thanks; but we have long since gone beyond the experimental stage. I was only trying a new bullet that I fancy the shape of. I ask your pardon for having given you a fright." He took her hand and kissed it. She beckoned to Hedwig as soon as it was released, and smiled kindly on him as she left the room with her servant to dress befittingly to show herself to Mademoiselle Rebecca. Had it been only her husband to face, she might have been content to look dusty with travel as she had to Antonino.

"How you delight that poor gentleman," observed Hedwig, between pity and admiration. "You would witch an angel."

"I am only practicing to enchant my husband, you dull creature!" said Césarine merrily. "He is a great man, and I have been proud of him from the first."

XIV

Truly a Man

Long after Madame Clemenceau had left the room, the Italian stood in the same position as he had taken after kissing her hand. The mild voice from the pallid but little changed beauty thrilled him as formerly, and went far towards making him as mad as he had been ten days before when she had dropped, like an extinguished star, out of that small system. In her absence, he had regained quiet and some coolness, and believed he had conquered the treasonable passion which threatened his benefactor with disgrace. Had she not disgraced him as it was; had she not run away with another lover?

Clemenceau had not said one word to his associate about the telegram from Paris, which he seemed not to believe, or of the note beginning: "The faithless one," by which Von Sendlingen had been warned of Gratian's absconding and which he instructed Hedwig to place where her master must see it. Hence, the view by Clemenceau of the stamping out of the Viscount-baron, for his accomplices had not let the chance pass when he stumbled into their ambush, in order to see if the Frenchman in jealous spite would assail him.

Clemenceau had recognized his wife and he divined that the lonely man making for the same point was the villain, without understanding into what deathpit he had fallen.

At the juncture of his being about hurrying after his wife, he heard the half-strangled wretch's outcry and the low appeal of humanity overpowering the hoarse summons of revenge in his bosom. But when he arrived at the broken footway bridge, all was over. A little farther, he fancied he saw a shadow in an osier bed, but when he waded to it, all was hushed. He called, but no sound responded. All seemed a vision—victim and assassins.

And his wife was flying, by the train which had merely stopped to take her up. As every resident is known at these suburban stations, he refrained from an inquiry which would have made him a laughing-stock.

Since Césarine had returned, the conflict of duty and passion would be resumed and he felt sure that he had been defeated before. Reflecting profoundly, he could come to no other conclusion than that he ought to shun the dangerous traitress.

As he lifted his head, less troubled after arriving at this resolution, he was not sorry to see that Clemenceau had silently entered the room.

"Oh, is it you, my dear master?" he exclaimed.

It was not easy on that placid brow to read whether he knew of Césarine's return or not.

"Well, are you satisfied with your test this morning?" inquired he. "Have you succeeded with the bullets of the new shape?"

"I believe so," answered Antonino, "for the modifications which you suggested, improved it in every point they dealt with. They go forth clean and the windage is much reduced."

"Is the range improved?"

"At fourteen hundred metres I put two elongated balls into an oak so deeply that I could not dig them out with my knife. They struck very closely to one another. It is a hundred metres greater distance. Inserting the bullets by the mass of twenty-five and firing the two took four seconds. I was less careful about marking where the others struck, and one that I discharged on my return near the house broke and went badly askew. With bullets made by regular moulders, such an accident should not happen."

"Have you any left? Let me see."

Antonino took two bullets from his waistcoat pocket; they were unlike the ordinary globules, and resembled the long, pointed cylinders of modern guns. With a pair of pocket plyers, he broke one to exhibit the interior to Clemenceau; it was composed of two metals in curiously shaped segments and a chamber in one end contained a loose ball of another and heavier metal, on the principle of the quick-silver enhancing the force of the blow of the "loaded" executioner's sword. All had a novel aspect, but the chief inventor was familiar with the arrangement.

"By the cavity in it I have reduced the weight of three to two," went on Antonino. "I am in hopes to put in fifty or sixty bullets at a time without making the arm too heavy, and that would suffice, considering that the replacement of the mass of projectiles requires no appreciable time, while the supply of explosive, liquefied air suffices for three hundred discharges. The repetition of the emissive force does not jar the gun, and the metal of our alloy does not show a strain although the gauge induces a pressure of fifty thousand pounds per square inch if it were accumulated."

"And the injection valve?"

"It works as easily by pressure on the disc, which replaces the trigger, perfectly."

"That was your idea."

"After you put me on the track," returned the Italian, gratefully. "Oh, I am still very ignorant in these matters."

"Not more than I, a few months ago. I had not handled a firearm until—" he checked himself and frowned; then, tranquilly resuming, he said: "Labor, and you will reach the goal!"

Antonino looked on silently as his instructor took the gun and inserted the bullet, but when he was going over to the open window, with the evident intention to fire off into the garden, he followed and laid his hand on his arm, saying animatedly:

"Do not fire!"

"Why not?" returned Clemenceau, but without astonishment. "We live in a desert since we have frightened our neighbors away. For two leagues around, nobody is about at this hour and everybody within our walls is accustomed to the noise of the gas exploding."

"Not everybody," remonstrated Antonino. "Madame Clemenceau has returned home and the sound frightens her because so strange."

"It is so. That's another matter," replied the inventor, putting the rifle down in the corner without haste.

"Did you know it? Have you seen her?" cried Antonino, struck by the remarkable unconcern of his master.

"I knew of it by seeing her, yes, as I was coming down stairs a while since—she was going to her rooms from this one, with her maid."

"It's a lucky thing that Mademoiselle Daniels refused to occupy them!" exclaimed Antonino. "Why did you not speak to your wife?"

"Because I can have nothing to say to her and she would speak to me nothing but lies," said Clemenceau in so severe and convinced a tone that the young man remained silent, hurt at the judgment pronounced upon his idol by its own high-priest. "What are you brooding over?" he inquired, after an embarrassing pause.

"My dear master, I think that I ought to ask leave of absence since I have finished the work of designing the bullet most fit for the gas-rifle."

"Do you ask leave of me, at your age, as of a schoolmaster?"

The relations between the adopted son and the architect, who had mistaken his bent and become an innovator in artillery, had been affectionate, and on the younger man's side respectful. He had never taken any serious steps without asking his consent.

"Well, where did you think of going?" asked Clemenceau.

"To Paris."

"To show the rifle and projectile complete? No, we can test the latter at the new series of firing experiments before the Ordnance Committee. The Minister of War and the Emperor will not thank you for disturbing them for so little. It was the great gun they wanted. They are wedded to the Chassepot for the soldier's gun and, besides, the government musket factories are opposed to so great a novelty."

"I need exercise—action—the open air," persisted the Italian.

Clemenceau shook his head. Only the day before, the young man had called himself the happiest soul in the world and did not wish to quit tranquil Montmorency.

"Well, after you have had your fling, would you hasten back?"

"I—I fear not, master," said he. "I daresay if you and M. Daniels should approve, I might have a situation to travel for the Clemenceau Rifle Company, for some months, in England or America—and explain the value of your invention."

"You wish to be my trumpeter, eh?" said the Frenchman, sadly smiling. "But what is to become of me during your absence and of M. Daniels? Remember that I have nobody to understand me, sympathize with me, become endeared to me, and aid me!"

"I, alone?" repeated the Italian, affected by the melancholy tone common to the man of one idea who must, to concentrate his thoughts, set aside other ties of union with his race.

"Do you doubt it?"

Antonino felt no doubt. He would be the most to be deplored among men if he were not fond of Clemenceau after all that he had done for him. He was an orphan vagrant, next to a beggar, when he had been housed by him, kept, and highly educated. Then, too, with a frankness not common among born brothers, the Frenchman had associated him in all his labors for the revolution in the science of artillery—the greatest since Bacon discovered gunpowder. All that he was, he owed to the man before him.

"Believe me, father," he said, earnestly, "I esteem and venerate you!"

"And yet you keep secrets from me!" reproached Clemenceau.

"I—I have no secrets."

"I see you are too serious."

ALEXANDRE DUMAS, FILS

"I am only sorrowful—sorrowful at quitting you."

"Why should you do it, I repeat?"

"I am never merry—happiness is not my portion," faltered Antonino, not knowing what answer to make.

"That's nothing. Better now than later! At your age, unhappiness is easily borne—it is only what the sporting gentlemen call a preliminary canter. Wait till you come to the actual race!"

"I am not fit to dwell with others—with grave, earnest men; I am too nervous and impressionable."

"Because you come of an excitable race, and your childhood was passed in too deep poverty. You will grow out of all that, gradually. Stay here; oh, keep with me, for I have need of you and you require a companion-soul, soothing like mine. The kind of disappointment you experience is not to be cured by change of place. You carry it with you, and distance increases and strengthens it, and whenever you meet the object again to whom was due the vexation you will perceive that you went on the journey for no good."

Antonino looked at the speaker as one regards the mind-reader who has answered to the point. Clemenceau fixed him with his serene, unvarying eyes, and continued, in an emotionless voice, like a statue, speaking:

"You are in love—and you love my wife."

Antonino started away and involuntarily lifted his hands in a position of defense. Averting his eyes and unclenching his fists, he muttered sullenly:

"What makes you suppose that?"

"I saw it was so."

At the end of a silence more burdensome than any before the younger man found his voice and, as though tears interfered with his utterance, said pathetically, and indistinctly:

"Do you not acknowledge, master, now, that I must go; for when I am far away, perhaps you will forgive the ingrate!"

Looking at the young man of two-and-twenty, Clemenceau knew by his own infatuation at the same tender age with the same woman, that he had nothing to forgive him for—little to reproach him. It was youth that was to blame, and it had loved. No matter who that Cytherean priestess was, he must have adored her whether sister, wife or daughter of dearest friend, teacher and paternal patron. But it was clear from the grief that had made the youth a melancholy man that he was honorable.

Grief is never, when the outcome of remorse, a useless or evil feeling. It is a fair-fighting adversary which has only to be overcome to be a sure ally, always ready to defend and protect its victor. In his own terse language, that of a mathematician and mechanician who knew no words of double meaning.

Clemenceau told the Italian this.

"With your youth and your grief, such a spirit as yours and such a friend as you have in me, Anto," he said, "you possess the weapons of Achilles."

Antonino thought he was mocking at him and frowned.

"You think I am sneering? Or merely laughing at you? Alas, it is a long while since I indulged in laughter. It was this woman, with whom you have fallen in love, who froze the laugh forever on my lips! she would have been the death of me if I had not overruled her and exterminated her within my breast. How I loved her! how I have suffered through her—enough to be our united portions of future pain—suffer you no more, therefore. You are too young, tender and credulous to try a fall with that creature. She must have divined long ago that you were enamored of her. She is not too clear-sighted in all things, but she sees such effects by intuition. It is very probable that she has returned to this house on your account, so suddenly. I could guess that she was on the eve of flight, but not that she would return. She always needs fresh sensations to make herself believe that she is alive, for she is more lifeless than those whom she robbed of life."

Antonino did not understand the allusion, for he had never felt less like dying than since Césarine had been seen again.

"I mean that she sends the chill of death into the soul, heart and brain of man, and it congeals the marrow in his bones!" said Clemenceau, energetically. "You may say that if she is a wicked woman and if, whatever her defense, her absence covers some evil step, I ought to separate from her. It is all the present state of the law allows. But while her absence would have prevented you, or another friend, from meeting her, still she would have borne my name. That name I am doubly bound to make honorable, for it was stained with blood—that of one of her ever-accursed race. My father won an illustrious name and, her ancestress, whom he married, was dragging it publically in the mud amid all the scandals of society, when he slew her on her couch of gilded infamy. Ashamed of this name—not because he was indicated under it, but because she had so vilified it—his greatest desire to the friends who visited him in the condemned cell, was to have me, his son, change it. They had me brought up at a distance under the name of Claudius Ruprecht. It might even have happened that another country than that of my birth would receive the glory which a heaven-sent idea is to bestow upon France. Now, I am more than ever determined that her venom shall not sully me. She may cause a little ridicule to arise, but that I can scorn. The laugh at Montmorency will not reach Paris, far less echo around the globe! For a long time I hoped to enlighten her and redeem her, but I have failed. But I am bound to enlighten you and save you, am I not? From the feeling you harbor can spring only an additional shame for Césarine, and certain, perhaps irreparable woe for you. Stop, turn about and look the other way. A man of twenty, who may naturally live another three-score years and work during two of them, who would talk to you of that nonsense, love's sorrow? That was all very well once, when the world revolved slowly and there was little to be done by the people who blocked nobody's way. But these are busy times and things to be done cannot wait till you finish loving and wailing, or till you die of a broken heart without having done anything for your fellow men."

"Bravo!" exclaimed the sympathetical and easily aroused Italian, grasping the speaker by the hand and pressing it with revived energy. "My excellent leader, you are right!"

"And by and by," said the other, with an effort, as though he had to master inward commotion, "when you win a prize from your own country and you look for household joys more agreeably to reward you, you may find one not far from here at this moment to be your wife. For, generally, the bane is near the antidote—the serpent is crushed under the heel next the beneficent plant which heals the bite."

"Rebecca?" questioned the young man in amazement. "But if I can read her heart as you do mine, master, Rebecca Daniels loves you."

"She admires me and pities me, Antonino," replied Clemenceau, hastily, as if wishful to elude the question. "She does not love me. Besides, that is of no consequence. I have no room for love again—always provided that I have once loved. Passion often has the honor of being confounded with the purer feeling, especially in the young. Did I love that monster—for she is a monster, Antonino—I might forgive, for love excuses everything—that is true love, but it is rare as virtue—common sense and all that is truth. To the altar of love, many are called, but few elected, and all are not fit.

"I see you are not convinced, because the dog that bit me is so shapely, and graceful and wears so silky a coat! Such dogs are mad and their bite in the heart is fatal and agonizing unless one at once applies the white hot cautery. The seam remains—from time to time it aches—but the victim's life is saved that he may save, serve, gladden his fellow men. Would you rather I should weep, or force a smile, and appear happy for a period? In any case, since I have cured the injury and she is in my house again, I shall not retaliate on her. But if she threatens to become a public danger—if she bares her poisonous fangs to harm my friend— my son—another—let her beware!"

"Master," stammered Antonino, beginning to see the temptress in the new light, as Felix had often shown him other objects to which he had been blind, "you may or may not judge her too harshly, but you certainly judge me too leniently. Better to let me go away, and far, or at least, since you began the revelation, make the evidence complete of your trust and esteem."

Clemenceau saw that the young man still believed in Césarine, but he did not care to tell him all he knew of her. Had he been told that she had encouraged Gratian to flee with her and had abandoned him at the first danger, without lifting a finger to save him, or her voice to procure him succor, he might loathe and hate her; but Clemenceau meant to say nothing. Such revelations, and denunciations are permissible alone to wrath, revenge, or despair, in the man whose heart is still bleeding from the wound made in it so that his outburst is sealed by his blood.

"No, Antonino, by my mouth no one shall ever know all that woman has done—or what victories I have won over myself—in severe wrestlings."

"I see you have forgiven her," said the Italian, advancing the virtue in which he was deficient.

"I have expunged her from my heart," answered Clemenceau firmly. "She is a picture on only one page of my life-book, and I do not open it there. Knowing my secret, you are the last person to whom I shall speak of Césarine's misdeeds. I wish your deliverance, like mine, to be owed to your will, but you are free and have been forewarned, so that you will have less effort to make than I. Let the scarlet woman go by and do not step across her path. Between two smiles, she will dishonor you or deal death to you! She slays like a dart of Satan. That is all you need know. But, as, indeed, you deserve a token of esteem and confidence from your frankness, affection and labors, I will give you one."

Having seated himself, he drew from an inner pocket a paper written in odd characters.

"The time of my giving you the proof of trust should make it more sacred and precious still. I have found the solution of the last problem over which we pored. You know that while we discovered the means of imprisoning the gas in a concentrated form of scarcely appreciable bulk, it was not always our obedient slave, we had the fear that sometimes it would not submit to being liberated by piecemeal but would now and then disrupt its containing chamber in impatience, and then the holder would certainly die, choked if the fragments of the gun had not fatally lacerated him. After many days and nights, I have found the simple means to render the gas innocuous except in the direction to which we direct its flow. I have written out the formula, in the minutest particulars and in the cipher which you and I alone understand. In the same way we two share the secret of this safe."

He handed Antonino a peculiar key and he went to unlock the coffer which had aroused Madame Clemenceau's curiosity.

"Lock it up with the other papers," concluded the inventor. "I appoint you its keeper while I live—my heir and the carrier out of the work after my decease, should I die before having proved what I consign there. What matters it now if my material form disappears when my spirit lives on in thee! Well," he said, as Antonino returned, after closing and fastening the chest, "do you need any farther proof of the confidence I have in you?"

Antonino grasped his hand and wrung it fondly When both had recovered calmness, they went on speaking of their work, which might be considered past the stage when the projector is racked by misgivings. They went into the breakfast-room together, prepared to bear the singular meeting with the errant wife whose return was so unexpected. But she preferred not to take the step so soon, and, as Rebecca also kept away, warned by Hedwig, who might appear at the board, the three men took their meal together.

XV

The Man of Many Masks

From dawn a stranger had been wandering about Montmorency. Armed with a large sun-umbrella and a Guid-Joanne, his copiously oiled black side-whiskers glistening in the sun, showing large teeth in a friendly grin to wayfarers of all degrees, one did not need to hear his strong accent of the people of Marseilles to know that he was a son of the South. Probably having made a fortune in shipping, in oils or wines, he was utilizing his holiday by touring in the north of his country, forced to admire, but still pugnaciously asseverating that no garden equalled his city park and no main street his Cannebiere. He seemed to have no destination in particular; he stopped here and there at random, and used a large and powerful field-glass, slung by a patent leather strap over his brawny shoulders, to study the points in the wide landscape. Now and then he made notes in his guide-book, but with a good-humored listlessness which would have disarmed the most suspicious of military detectives. On descending the hillside, he did not scruple to stop to chat with a nurse maid or two out with the children, and to open his hand as freely to give the latter some silver as he had opened his heart to the girl—all with an easy, hearty laugh, and the oily accent of his fellow-countrymen.

He exchanged the time of day with the clerks hurrying to the railroad station; he did not disdain to ask the roadmender, seated on a pile of stones, how his labor was getting on, and where he would work next week; he leaned on the gate to listen as if enrapt to the groom and gardener of a neighbor of Clemenceau's, regretting that the hubbub of cracking guns and other ominous explosions was driving their master from home. Then, rattling his loose silver, and whistling a fisher's song, which he must have picked up off the Hyéres, he paused before the gateway of the house which had become the Ogre's Cave of Montmorency, and read half aloud the placard nailed on a board to a tree and announcing that the property was in the open market.

"The Reine-Claude Villa, eh!" muttered he to himself. "The name pleases me! I must go in and see if it is worth the money. To say nothing," he added still more secretly, "of the mistress having returned this morning. I wonder how she had the courage to walk along the road in the dawn, when she might have met the ghost of our poor Gratian von Linden-hohen-Linden!"

This acquaintance with the unpublished story of Madame Clemenceau rather contradicted the aspect and accent of a Marseillais, and, although the black whiskers did not remind one of Von Sendlingen when we saw him at Munich, than of his clear shaven, wrinkled face as the Marchioness de Letourlagneau pianist, it was not so with the burly figure, more robust than corpulent.

He opened the gate without ringing and stepped inside on the gravel path winding up to the pretty but not lively house.

"Attention," he muttered suddenly, in a military tone. "Here is our own little spy in the camp—Hedwig. It will be as well she does not recognize me without my cue."

Running his large red hand over his whiskers, he jovially accosted the girl, after adjusting his formidable accoutrement field-glass, guide-book, case and heavy watch chain, adorned with a compass and a pedometer. She stood on the porch before the windows of the room into which her mistress had entered so early in the morning.

"What do you seek, monsieur?" she challenged, after an unfavorable glance upon the stranger who had greatly offended her idea of dignity by not ringing and waiting at the portals to be officially admitted.

"Pardon me, young lady," the man said, with the southern accent so strong that a flavor of garlic at once pervaded the air, "but I did not think that your papa and mamma and the family were in the house, seeing that it is for sale."

"Young lady? My papa? Let me tell you that I am the housemaid here and if you have intended to jest—"

"Jest! purchasing a house, and rather large gardens, is no jest, not in the environs of Paris!" returned the visitor. "Is it you who are to show the property?"

"No. If you will wait, I will tell master," said Hedwig, not at all flattered by being pretendedly taken for "the daughter of the house."

She turned round, made the half-circuit of the house, and entered the breakfast-room where the three gentlemen were still in debate.

"A gentleman, to see the house, with a view to purchase, eh?" said Clemenceau. "Very well, I will go into the drawing-room and speak with him. Is your mistress having a nap?"

"No, monsieur."

"Then, be so good as to tell her that somebody has come about the house, and as such inquirers are sure to be supplied by their wives with formidable lists of questions about domestic details, I should be obliged by her coming down to send the person away satisfied."

He followed Hedwig on the way up through the house as far as the drawing-room door, where his path branched off. Entering, he threw open the double window-sashes and politely asked the gentleman to make use of this direct road, with an apology for suggesting it. But he had seen at a glance that this kind of happy-go-lucky tourist was not of the ceremonious strain.

"It is you, monsieur," began the latter, taking the seat pointed out to him and immediately swinging one leg, mounted on the other knee, with the utmost nonchalance, "it is you who are the proprietor of this pretty place?"

"Yes; my name is Clemenceau, at your service."

"Then, monsieur, I am—where the plague have I put my card-case—I am Guillaume Cantagnac, lately in business as a notary, but for the present, at the head of an enterprise for the purchase of landed estates, and their development by high culture for the ground and superior structures instead of their antiquated houses. I read in the *Moniteur des Ventes*, and on the placard at your gates, that you are willing to dispose of this residence and the land appertaining thereunto. I am not on business this morning, but taking a little pleasure-trip—no, not pleasure-trip—God forbid I should find any pleasure now! I mean a little tour for distraction after a great sorrow that has befallen me."

The stout man, though he could have felled a bull with a blow of his leg-of-mutton fist, seemed about to break down in tears. But, burying his empurpled nose in a large red handkerchief, he passed off his emotion in a potent blast which made the ornaments on the mantel-shelf quake, and resumed in an unsteady voice:

"I would have made a note and deferred to another day seeing the property you offer and learning its area, value, situation, advantages and defects—for there is always some flaw in a terrestrial paradise, ha, ha! But your hospitable gate was on the latch—such an inviting expression was on the face of a rather pretty servant girl on your porch—faith! I could not resist the temptation to make the acquaintance of the happy owner of this Eden! and lo! I am rewarded by the power to go home to Marseilles and tell my companion domino-players in the Café Dame de la Garde that I saw the renowned constructor of the new cannon—M. Felix Clemenceau, with whom the Emperor has spoken about the defense of our beloved country!"

Clemenceau could only bow under this deluge of words.

"M. Clemenceau, will you honor me with the clasp of the hand?"

The host allowed his hand to disappear from view in the enormous one presented, timidly.

"Ah! in case of the universal European War, they are talking about, France will have need of such men as you!"

The embarrassing situation for the modest inventor was altered for the better by the entrance of Antonino, who darted a keen glance upon the genial stranger.

"How do you do?" cried the latter, nodding kindly. "Your son, I suppose, M. Clemenceau?"

"By adoption. I am hardly of the age to have a son as old as that!"

"I beg your pardon! I see now, that it is brain-work that has worn you out a little. But, bless you, that will all get smoothed out when you begin to enjoy the windfall of fortune! I dare say now you are selling out because the Emperor offers you a piece of one of his parks, wanting you to live near him. And I presume this bright young gentleman is of the same profession? Has he, too, invented a great gun?"

"He is the author of several not inconsiderable inventions," replied Clemenceau for Antonino, who was not delighted with the stranger's ways, had gone to look out of the nearest window, although it necessitated his rudely turning his back on him.

"Any cannon among them?"

"No, M. Cant—Cant—"

"Cantagnac—"

"Cantagnac; only a very notable bullet of novel shape."

"A bullet, dear me! a bullet! a novel bullet! what an age we are living in, to be sure! I applaud you, young man, and you must allow me to say to my companions in the Café de la Garde at Marseilles, that I shook the hand of the inventor of the new bullet!" But as Antonino did not make a responsive movement, he had to add, unabashed: "before I go, I mean! But allow me to say, gentlemen, that though I am only a commonplace notary, and a retired one, at that, ha, ha! a buyer of houses to modernize, and land to improve in cultivation; though lowly, and very ill-informed on the great questions which occupy you, yet I venture to assert that I take the greatest interest in your labors. I would give half—aye, three-quarters of my possessions toward your success. My life should be yours if it were useful in any way, although that would be a small gift, as it has no value in my own eyes. I had a son, M. Clemenceau—an only son, tall, dark, handsome and, though he took after me, bright—like this young gentleman of talent here!" He flourished the voluminous red handkerchief again. "In an evil hour, I let him go on a holiday excursion and he chose the Rhine. His boyish gallantry caused him to champion a waitress on a steamboat, whom a bullying German officer of the Landsturm had chucked under the chin. High words were exchanged— my boy challenged the giant, who did not understand our way among gentlemen of settling such matters—he knocked my hopeful one overboard—no, gentlemen, he was not drowned, but he never recovered from the mortification of being laughed at. He came home but to die— in the following year, poor, sensitive soul! His mother never held her head up again, and I—" he blew his nose with a tremendous peal, "I—I beg your pardon for forgetting my business, again."

"Not at all!" exclaimed Clemenceau, while Antonino, angry at having misjudged the bereaved parent, offered him the hand he had previously refused.

"I thank you both," said M. Cantagnac, hastening to dry his tears which might have seemed of the crocodile sort when they had time to remember he had been a notary. "This is not my usual bearing! Three years ago I was called the Merry One, for I was always laughing, but now"—he gave a great gulp at a sob like a rosy-gilled salmon taking in a fly and abruptly said:

"So you want to sell your house, with all belongings? Which are—"

"About twelve acres, mostly young wood, but some rocky ground ornamental enough, which will never be productive. Do you mind getting the plan, Antonino? It is hanging up in my study."

Antonino went out, not sorry to be beyond earshot of the boisterous negotiator.

"Young wood, eh?" repeated the latter, "humph! lots of stony ground! ahem! yet it is pretty and so near town. I wonder you sell it."

"I want ready money," returned Clemenceau, bluntly.

"So we all do, ha, ha! But you surely could raise on it by mortgage."

"I have tried that."

"The deuce you have! That's strange, when the Emperor said your discovery—"

"It is a gold mine, but like gold mines, it has plunged the discoverer into debt."

"I dare say it would! and I suppose it is not so certain-sure as the newspapers assert—"

"I beg your pardon, it is beyond all doubt," replied Clemenceau, sharply.

XVI

Strike Not Woman, Even with Roses

S top a bit," said M. Cantagnac, pulling a newspaper out of his pocket. "This is a journal I picked up in the cars. I always do that. There is sure to be some passenger to throw them down and so I never buy any myself when I am traveling, ha, ha! Well, in this very sheet, there is a long article about you. It is called 'The Ideal Cannon' and the writer declares that the experiment was a great hit, ha, ha! and he undertakes to explain the new system."

Clemenceau smiled contemptuously. He was not one of those to make a secret public property on which a nation's salvation might depend. In such momentous matters, he would have had arsenals, armories, navy yards and military museums labeled over the door:

"Speech is silver, silence is of gold;
Death unto him who dares the tale unfold!"

"Ah, he wouldn't know everything, of course. However, he makes out that you obtain the wonderful result by fixing essential oils in a special magazine and that you managed to project a solid shot to the prodigious distance of—of—" he referred to the newspaper—"fifteen miles by means of—of—I do not understand these jaw-breaking scientific terms. Is it not nitroglycerine?"

"I do not use them myself," remarked Clemenceau, dryly.

"But he adds—look here!" continued the worthy Man from Marseilles, regretfully, "that what you managed to perform with your model and material, specially prepared by yourself, could not be attained on the proper scale in a war campaign. He goes on to say that the scientific world await the explanation of the means to obtain such power as, heretofore, the pressure of liquefied gases has been but some five hundred pounds to the square inch, about a tenth of that of explosives now used. It is admitted, however, that there may be something in your increase of effectiveness by reiterated emissions—" He began to stammer, as if he were speaking too glibly, but his auditor took no alarm. "He continues that, up to this day, gases have failed as propelling powers from their instantaneous explosions."

"The writer is correct," said Clemenceau, a little warmed, "or, rather, he had foundation for his criticism when he wrote. The powerful agent was not perfectly controllable at the period of my last official experiments, but that is not the case at present. This enormous, almost incalculable power is so perfectly under my thumb, monsieur, that not only is it manageable in the largest cannon, but it is suitable for a parlor pistol, which a child might play with."

"Wonderful!" exclaimed Cantagnac, with undoubted sincerity, for his eyes gleamed.

"In solving that last enigma, I found the power became more strong when curbed. Consequently, the gun that would before have carried fifteen miles, may send twenty, and the ball, if not explosible, might ricochet three."

"Wonderful!" cried the Marseillais again, who displayed very deep interest in the abstruse subject for a retired notary.

"The bullet, or shell, or ball—all the projectiles are perfected now!" went on Clemenceau, triumphantly, "and were I surrounded by a million of men, or had I an impregnable fortress before me, a battery of my cannon would finish the struggle in not more than four hours."

"Why, this is a force of nature, not man's work," said Cantagnac, through his grating teeth, as though the admiration were extracted from him. "I do not see how any army or any fort could resist such instruments."

"No, monsieur, not one."

"Would not all the other nations unite against your country?"

"What would that matter, when, I repeat, the number of adversaries would not affect the question?"

"What a dreadful thing! I beg your pardon, but I go to church and I have had 'Love one another!' dinned into my ears. What is to become of that precept, eh?"

"It is what I should diffuse by my cannon," returned Clemenceau.

"By scattering the limbs of thousands of men, ha, ha!" but his laugh sounded very hollow, indeed.

"Not so; by destroying warfare," was the inventor's reply. "War is impious, immoral and monstrous, and not the means employed in it. The more terrible they are, the sooner will come the millennium. On the day when men find that no human protection, no rank, no wealth, no influential connections, nothing can shield them from destruction by hundreds of thousands, not only on the battlefield, but in their houses, within the highest fortified ramparts, they will no longer risk their country, homes, families and bodies, for causes often insignificant or dishonest. At present, all reflecting men who believe that the divine law ought to rule the earth, should have but one thought and a single aim: to learn the truth, speak it and impress it by all possible means wherever it is not recognized. I am a man who has frittered away too much of his time on personal tastes and emotions, and I vow that I shall never let a day pass without meditating upon the destination whither all the world should move, and I mean to trample over any obstacle that rises before me. The time is one when men could carouse, amuse themselves, doze and trifle—or keep in a petty clique. The real society will be formed of those who toil and watch, believe and govern."

"I see, monsieur, that you cherish a hearty hatred for the enemies of the student and the worker," said the ex-notary, not without an inexplicable bitterness, "and that you seek the suppression of the swordsman."

"You mistake—I hate nobody," loftily answered Clemenceau. "If I thought that my country would use my discovery to wage an unjust war, I declare that I should annihilate the invention. But whatever rulers may intend, my country will never long carry on an unfair war and it is only to make right prevail that France should be furnished with irresistible power."

While listening, Cantagnac had probably considered that raillery was not proper to treat such exaltation, for he changed his tone and noisily applauded the sentiments.

"Capital, capital! that's what I call sensible talk! And do you believe that I would leave a man, a patriot, in temporary embarrassment when he has discovered the salvation of our country? Why, this house will become a sight for the world and his wife to flock unto! I am proud that I have stood within the walls and I shall tell the domino-players of the Café—but never mind that now! To business! Between ourselves, are you particularly fond of this house?"

"It is my only French home, where I brought my bride, where my child was born—where the great child of my brain came forth—"

"Enough! we can arrange this neatly. It is my element to smooth matters over. Something is in the air about a company to 'work' your minor inventions in firearms, eh? good! I engage, from my financial connections, to find you all funds required; I shall charge twenty-five per cent. on the profits, and never interfere with your scientific department, which I do not understand, anyway. There is no necessity of our seeing one another in the business, but I do want to put my shoulder to the wheel—*wheel* of Fortune, eh? ha, ha!" and he rubbed his large hands gleefully till they fairly glowed.

There was no resisting openness like this, and Clemenceau heartily thanked the volunteer "backer," as is said in monetary circles.

"That's very kind; but the proposal has previously been made to me by an old friend, an Israelite who also has connections with the principal bankers. But these transactions take time, on a large scale and to embrace the world. Meanwhile, although he would readily and easily find me temporary accommodation, the pressure on me is not acute enough for me to accept a helping hand."

"I understand: you would not be in difficulties if you were another kind of man. Let us say no more about it. As the company will be a public one, I suppose, I can take shares. About this mortgage over our heads, is some bank holding it?"

"Well, no; my wife has it, as part of the marriage portion, or rather my gift. I have sent for her to step down to discuss the matter with you."

"Happy to see the lady," said Cantagnac, pulling out his whiskers and adjusting the points of his collar. "We will discuss it, with an eye to your interests, monsieur."

It was clear that M. Cantagnac had not enchanted Antonino, for he had taken care not to bring the plan of the house; it was brought, but by another hand. On seeing the lady, the Marseillais bowed with exaggerated politeness of the old school and stammered his compliments.

"No, no;" Clemenceau hastened to say, "this is not the lady of the house, but a guest who, however, will show you the place."

It was Rebecca Daniels. As always happens with the Jews, whose long, oval faces are not improved by mental trouble, she looked less captivating than when she had shone as the star of the Harmonista Music-hall; but, nevertheless, she was, for the refined eye, very alluring. She accepted the task imposed on her with a gentle smile, although it was evident that in her quick glance she had summed up the visitor's qualities without much favor for him.

While Cantagnac was bowing again and fumbling confusedly with his hat, Rebecca laid the plan on the table and whispered to Clemenceau:

"Do you know that she is here again?"

He nodded, whereupon her features, which had been animated, fell back into habitual calm.

"She sends word by Hedwig, whom I intercepted, that she wants to see you before seeing this purchaser of the house. I need not urge you to keep calm?"

"No!"

"Come this way, please, monsieur," said Rebecca, lightly, as if fully at ease, and she led Cantagnac out of the room.

Left to himself, with the notification of the important interview overhanging him, the host pondered. He had at the first loved Rebecca, and it was strange to him now that he had let Césarine outshine her. He had acted like an observer, who takes a comet for a planet shaken out of its course. Since he loved the Jewess with a holier flame than ever the Russian kindled, he perceived which was the true love. This is not an earthly fire, but a divine spirit; not a chance shock, but the union of two souls in unbroken harmony.

It is possible that Von Sendlingen in transmitting to Clemenceau the notice by the butler's wife, that the Viscount Gratian was to aid her in flight, but which as plainly revealed the wife's flight, had expected the angered husband to execute justice on the betrayer. Human laws could have absolved him if he had slain the couple at sight, but Clemenceau, after the example of his father, had resolved not to transgress the divine mandate again, even in this cause. He would have separated the congenial spirits of cunning and deceit, but not by striking a blow, and the rebuke to Césarine would have been so scathing she would never have had the impudence to see him again. Not by murder did he mean to liberate himself.

On seeing that heaven had taken the parting of the gallant and the wanton into its hand, he had simply forbore to intervene. On the one hand, he let Gratian's mysterious and stealthy assassins stifle him and the other, Césarine, run to the railroad station unhailed. The one deserved death as the other deserved oblivion.

This woman was of the world and would be a clod when no longer living—her essence would remain to inspirit some other evil woman—the same malignity in a beautiful shape which appeared in Lais, Messalina, Lucrezia Borgia, the Medici, Ninon, Lecouvreur, Iza, not links of a chain, but the same gem, a little differently set.

But Rebecca's was an ethereal spirit eternal. Thinking of her he could believe himself young and comely again and loving forever in another sphere. This was the being whom he would eternally adore, whether he or she were the first to quit the earth.

Here lay the consolation. Césarine, like all evil, was transient; Rebecca, like all good, everlasting.

"Let her come," said he at last, lifting his head slowly and no longer troubled. "She need not fear. I shall bear in mind the Oriental proverb Daniels quoted: 'Do not beat a woman, even with roses!'"

Hardly were the words formed in his mind than his wife appeared as though by that mind reading, frequent in married couples—she had waited for this assurance of her personal safety to be mentally formed.

In the short time given her toilet, she had performed wonders. Perhaps, with a surprising effort of her will, she had snatched some rest, for her eyes wore the fresh, pellucid gleam after prolonged slumber. Her cheeks were smooth and by artifice, seemed to wear the virginal down. Easy and graceful as ever, she affected a slight constraint, which agreed with a pretence of avoiding his glances.

"You must be astonished to see me!" she exclaimed, for he did not say a word of greeting.

No man could have looked less astonished, and, with the greatest evenness of tone, he answered:

"You ought to know that nothing you do astonishes me."

"But I remember—I wrote you a long letter explaining my absence and the necessity of my sudden departure—the despatch from my poor uncle's secretary—I ordered it to be given you—it explained my sudden departure—"

"Hedwig gave me the paper," he said shortly.

"But my letter, saying I had nursed him to convalescence and had fallen ill myself? You had time to reply but you did not do so."

"I received no letter," he said, like a speaking machine.

"Dear, dear, how could that be!" she muttered, tapping her foot on the head of the tiger-skin rug.

"Perhaps it arises from your never writing me any," he said, but without bitterness.

"Oh, I could swear—"

"It is of no consequence either way."

"Since you did not reply, I came to you although it was at a great risk. I would not tell you that I was leaving a sickroom for fear it would fill you with too great pain or too great hope."

"How witty you are!"

"Would you not be happy if I died?"

"If you were in a dying state, somebody might have written for you—Madame Lesperon or your uncle," speaking as if the persons were fabulous creatures.

"Oh, my granduncle is well known at the Russian Embassy, and Madame and M. Lesperon remember your lamented father distinctly."

He bit his lip as if he detested hearing his father spoken of by her.

"Madame wanted to write to you—she expected you to come for me, like any other husband, but I knew you were not like other husbands, and would not come."

She was sincere; women always speak out when boldness is an excuse.

"You mistake," he interrupted, "I would have come, under the belief that on your death bed, you would have confession to make or desires to express which a husband alone should hear."

"What do you suppose?" cried Césarine, trying to forget that the speaker must have seen the death of her lover—whether he connived at it or not—and her flight, whether he facilitated it or not.

"I do not suppose anything, but I remember and I forsee."

"Do you mean to say that you do not feel ill-will because I have come back?"

"Madame Clemenceau, this house is ours—as much yours as mine. That is why I asked you to come down here, for it is necessary to sell it."

"Why am I charged with the business?"

"Because you have an interest in it. Half of all I own is yours."

"But you long ago repaid my share, and generously!"

"Not in the eyes of the law, and it pleases me that you should do this."

"But I do not need anything. My uncle was pleased at my nursing him back to health; his children have been unkind to him, and he has transferred to me some property in France, a handsome income! Grant to me a great pleasure—of which I am not worthy," she went on tearfully, "but you will have the more merit, then! Let me lend you any sum of which you have need."

"I thank you, but I have already refused a thousand times the amount from an unsullied hand!" returned Clemenceau, emphatically.

"That Jewess'!" she exclaimed, with a great change in her bearing.

"Hush! strangers present!" and in uttering this talismanic cue between married people, he pointed to the shadow on the curtains.

Rebecca had concluded her pilotage of M. Cantagnac and it was he whom Clemenceau soon after presented to his wife.

ALEXANDRE DUMAS, FILS

"Let me add, M. Cantagnac, that you must be my guest as long as you stay at Montmorency, for the hotels are conducted solely for the excursionists who come out of Paris and their accommodations would not please you. You are expected to sit down to dinner with us at one o'clock, country fashion and I will order a bedroom ready also."

"Gracious heavens! you are really too good!" exclaimed Cantagnac, lifting his hands almost devoutly.

XVII

Demon and Arch-Demon

After one sharp slighting look at the visitor, Madame Clemenceau had withdrawn her senses within herself, so to say, to come to a conclusion on the singular conduct of her husband. His cold scorn daunted her, and filled her with dread. Had not the Jewess been on the spot, whom she believed to be a rival once more, however high was her character and Hedwig's eulogy, she would have prudently fled again without fighting. She had the less reason to stay, as the house was to be sold, in a manner of speaking, from under her feet.

Yet the Marseillais was worth more than a passing glance. When alone with the lady, whom he regarded steadfastly, a radical change took place in his carriage, and he who had been so easy and oily became stiff, stern and rigid. It was the attitude no longer of a secret agent, wearing the mien and mask of his profession, but of a military spy, who stands before a subordinate when disguise is superfluous.

"Truly, she is more bewitching than when I first knew her," he muttered between his close teeth, as if he admired with awe and suppressed breath. "What a pretty monster she is!"

Feeling that his view was weighing upon her, Madame Clemenceau suddenly looked up. It seemed to her that something in the altered and insolent bearing was not unknown to her but the recollection was hazy, and the black whiskers perplexed.

"Did you speak, monsieur?" she said, to give herself countenance.

"I spoke nothing," he replied still in the smooth accent which was not familiar to her. "A man of business like myself, feels bound, if he has any natural turning that way, to become a physiognomist and thought-reader in order not to pay too dearly for bargains; I am happy to say that I rarely blunder."

"Then you can read my disposition?" exclaimed Césarine mockingly.

"I knew it before."

"Indeed! then you would do me a great service, monsieur, if you would tell me how it strikes you, as an average man. For I assure you," she went on, taking a seat without pointing out one to him, "that some days I do not understand myself, a most humiliating thing, though ancient wisdom acknowledged that the hardest thing is self-knowledge."

"If you authorize me to be outspoken, madame, I will enlighten you," returned Cantagnac.

"Do not let me be in your way!" impertinently.

"It is the most simple thing, for your entire character is described in these four words: venal, ferocious, frivolous and insubmissive!"

She sprang to her feet with quivering lips and flashing eyes, while he, like a statue, lowered upon its pedestal, calmly sank upon an arm-chair. Then, looking round and listening to make certain that they had no observers, he leaned both elbows on the table and fixed his sea-blue eyes on the startled lady.

"Kaiserina!" he said in a commanding voice, without the least softening with that southern suavity, "for how much do you want to sell me secretly, your husband's invention?"

The altered voice appeared not at all strange, but the words were so unexpected that she merely stared in bewilderment while he had even more deliberately to repeat them. Deeply frightened by this mystery which in vain she tried to solve, she forced a laugh.

"Oh, it is no jest—I am one of the most serious of men," proceeded Cantagnac, "as becomes one of the busiest."

She looked at him like a fawn, which, having never seen a human being, is suddenly peered upon in the lair by the hunter.

"You want to know who I am, speaking to you in this style? See my card on the table there—it says I am Cantagnac, the agent, modest but passing for rather subtle, of a private and limited company recently established with a cash capital fully paid up of several millions of *fredericks*—for, to tell the plain facts to you—the obtaining for its profit the ideas, inventions and discoveries of others. In short, we, who used to despise mental fruits, see that it is the most profitable of trades to work genius. As soon as we see, learn, or even scent that an important thing is being produced anywhere in the world, we hurry to the spot and by one means or another—money, cunning, persuasion, main force, if needs must, we make ourselves master of what we must have if we mean to be the world's rulers. With a European war impending, even a lady will see at once of what value an invention is, like M. Clemenceau's."

"In plain language, you are proposing to me an infamous deed!" she exclaimed with scathing irony which failed to scare the other.

"I am proposing a matter of business. Where are you going?"

"Straight to my husband—whose confidence you have imposed on by some deception."

"Dear madame, do not do what you would eternally deplore," said Cantagnac quietly, and motioning with his broad hand for her to be seated again. "I deceived your husband with a bit of character acting which you would, I think, have applauded, as you were once on the stage—the music hall stage, at least."

She sat down, as if this allusion had stunned her.

"His secret is indispensable to my company and I was given instructions to try to obtain it, by surprise and for nothing, if possible. Without it, many another purchase of ours made at great expense, would become utterly useless. From an incomplete acquaintance with your husband, I feared I could do nothing with him; from a study of him here, at a later period, I doubted still more; and, having spoken with him, I am sure."

A previous acquaintance with Clemenceau? It was a ray of light, but still Césarine, who did not cease to stare at him, failed to identify him with a figure in her past. Was this only a new phase of a Proteus?

"Clemenceau is no longer the frank and enthusiastic student but a man of talent and feeling who has found his true course. In what concerns the revelation he has had from science, he is reserved and circumspect. Happily, man that is borne of woman, however great, if a simpleton and an idealist, almost always is the prey of the sex in one form or another. When they escape feminine influence, they are impregnable, and strong measures must be employed."

"Strong measures," repeated Césarine, shuddering at the icy, passionless tone like a lecturer's.

"They must be blotted off the book of life—and it is always painful to have to proceed to such extremities. It is frequent, very—and ninety-nine times in the hundred, we run up against the woman for whom a great magistrate advised the search whenever a crime is perpetrated."

"It would appear that you expect to induce me to commit that crime!" sneered the woman, pale but rebellious.

"We have no need to induce you, dear madame, for we can constrain you."

"Constrain me!" repeated the woman savagely and tossing her head with pride. "If you really knew my nature, you would not say that. You might tell me how?"

"Really know you? you shall judge for yourself. In your marriage certificate, you are described as of the Vieradlers, but your eagle is not the German one—it is the Polish. The women of your race are distinguished for beauty, when young, and freedom in love at all times. Your grandma has a volumnious chronicle of scandal all to herself, but her glory is thrown into the shade by the peculiar celebrity enjoyed rather briefly by her favorite daughter, La Belle Iza, that one of the Sirens of Paris who has, under the present Empire, lured the most men to wreck. This was your aunt. Her sister, your mother, quite as beautiful, was rescued at an early hour from her mother's manoeuvres to 'place' her, as she called it, and for this loss, the indignant old lady vowed a kind of unnatural vengeance, to be visited on the child of her who had offended her by remaining in the path of virtue. This child is the woman before me. Oh, it is useless to look at me like that!" he grimly said, with the perplexed air of a man with no ear for music who listens to a music-box delighting others. "Pure wasted labor! The old lady, who had fallen from her high estate where Iza had lifted her, and was ordered out of the capital for extorting hush-money upon her daughter's stock of love-letters, the old lady became a queen—a queen of the disreputable classes. In Munich, sleepy old town where superstitions linger and the women are as besotted with ignorance as the men with beer, she ruled the beggars and vagabonds. It was there that fate led you and you fell under her hand. She pretended to befriend you, for even so young, you promised to have power by your charms, renewing those she had never forgotten in her lost Iza. No one consulted the Almanack de Gotha when you were launched on an admiring society as one of the Vieradlers. You soon won a great reputation for freshness of wit and coquetry in all South Germany. In plain words, you could not see a man come into the drawing-room without wishing to make him fall in love with you. We want to monopolize genius—you to monopolize the love of man. You have the mania of loving, more common than it is suspected, especially by those who would have us believe that good society is a fold where snowy lambs are led about from the cradle to the butcher's shambles, by pastors carrying crooks decked with sky blue ribbons. The feeling is a craving in you—an involuntary and invincible instinct which was to have its inevitable end. You turned from a man who sincerely loved you to make a conquest of another whose heart was engaged."

"Stop!" interrupted Césarine, triumphantly for she had detected genuine feeling the last tone used by the living enigma. "I know you now! you are the man whom you say really loved me. Down with the masks! You are—"

"Not so loud!"

"You are Major von Sendlingen!"

"Say 'Colonel' and you will be exact. Yes; I am the lover whom you cast off in favor of the student Ruprecht, as this Clemenceau was called when he pottered about Europe, sketching ruined doorways and broken windows and dreamed of architectural structures. A man whom destiny had chosen to be the greatest demolisher of the age! what sarcasm!"

"Well, you should be the last to complain! Was it like devotion to me that you should try to abduct La Belle Stamboulane in the public street?

"To remove her from your path! She was your rival in the music hall! Love her, love a Jewess? You do not understand men—you fancy they are put here for your pleasure, safeguard and redemption. An error! We are neither your joy or your punishment. Let that pass. You married the student Ruprecht who turned out to be your cousin Felix Clemenceau. For a time you played the part of the idolizing young wife admirably. You never reproached his father's head for the murder of your aunt and he said never a word about the old beggar-sovereign Baboushka. In your gladness at having stolen the man away from Fraulein Daniels, I believe you imagined that it was love you felt. Not a bit of it! Love is the sun of the soul—all light, heat, motion and creativeness! there are no more two loves than two suns. There may be two or many passions, but not two loves. If a man loved twice, it would not be love!"

The hard man spoke so tenderly that his hearer dared not scoff.

"He ran through your witchery after a while, but he built his hopes upon maternity. You had a child but you connived at its death, if you did not deal the stroke."

How accurately Sendlingen had measured this woman! Another would have cried out against him at this accusation—or burst into tears and so disarmed a less adamantine man. She did not blanch; she did not lift her hand to cover her unaltered features, but listened as idly as she would to the last plaint of the fool who might blown out his brains at her feet. The false Cantagnac pursued in his natural voice, rancid and imperious, rolling out the gutturals like a heavy wagon thundering over an old road.

"It follows, madame, that if you run to your husband at a faster gait than you took to run away with the Baron of Linden, to inform him

ALEXANDRE DUMAS, FILS

of my proposition, I will tell him what you hear—I will accuse you of infanticide, of unfaithfulness—"

"He knows that!" exclaimed the woman with irony and in defiance. "Ask him, if you do not believe."

"Impossible."

"He would not say a word to anybody, and I would not have confessed only I was driven to it."

"And he forgave you?"

"All!"

"He is very grand; and few men of my acquaintance would not at least have caned you smartly. However, it was not long after the 'removal' of your child, to put it mildly, that you threw yourself into the swim of distractions, such as were to be had hereabouts. The old marchioness' circle soon surrounded you; she was one of my company's instruments, and from that time we counted on you as a coadjutrix some day."

"On me!"

"Precisely! to whom should we look for aid and complicity in our concealed and wary work but to the embodiment of permanent and domestic corruption? You are merely an impulse—we are a policy, and you will be our bondwoman. Ah, we are merely men—not fools, scoundrels or gods like your husband, for only such would tolerate depravity like yours."

"He is like a god," said Césarine, trembling, in a low, hushed voice. "When he speaks, it seems to me that it is what people call conscience."

"How long is it since you acknowledged this superiority?" sneered the sham Marseillais.

"Too short a while, alas! some few minutes," sighed she.

"Well, granting he is at least a demi-god, he is a power which we have an interest in destroying. Hercules became a nuisance to neglectful stable-keepers, and like conservative institutions. Let us have done with him. But, first, the final training of yourself. I repeat that the marchioness' house was the rendezvous at the gates of Paris, where we assembled our bearers of intelligence. Under cover of chit-chat and vocal-waltzes, we heard reports and issued orders. It was necessary to link you to us and we employed our foremost captivator, the dandy of two countries, the international Lothario, the Viscount-baron Gratian von Linden-hohen-Linden-*cum* de Terremonde. Luckily, too, he had been at the same period as myself, smitten with your vernal charms, and he entered upon his amorous mission with gusto. You believed him very wealthy, but let me tell you that the cash he really had under hand was our petty expense fund. Judge by that what a capital we control!" exclaimed Von Sendlingen proudly. "Our poor Gratian the double dealer, seemed not to be loved by the gods any more truly than by his goddess here present, for she let him, unassisted, be thrust down, on falling through a broken bridge, into the mire of a rivulet visible from your window. There he breathed his last. Fit death for a traitor! For our corporation, the untimely, unmanageable passion of this athletic fop might have had grave consequences, and for you. We did not find the money on his person only a pocketbook stuffed with rubbish, as if he were the victim of some gross deception. But, have no fear, Madame, we are not going to claim the sum from you, we prefer to let you regard it as a payment on account. We intend you no mischief, and we intended you none, then; we might have stopped your flight—that is, I might have done so, but I only threw myself across your path after you ran on, to stay your husband from pursuing you."

"You were there?" she stammered, more and more frightened at the vastness of the serpent which involved her with its coils, and which was so careless about the loss of its golden scales.

"Enough! all is well that ends well! You will serve us?"

"But I have repented!"

"Nonsense! you returned home because your husband was suddenly enriched above your dreams. Your repentance was simply a prompting of moral hygiene for you to take rest before a new and less unlucky flight. You had the instinctive warning that to the greatly successful inventor, the modern king or knowing man—for civilization has come round the circle to the point where savagery commenced and the wise man rules—to the wizard, power, riches, beauty, all gravitate. Your husband would be courted; duchesses would sue him to place their husbands or gallants on the board of his company—the dark-eyed charmer whom you ousted in the Munich music hall and whom you foresaw to be your eternal rival, might meet him again. With you beside him, she might be repulsed—with you distant, he would surrender at discretion. What a triumph for your self-conceit and banquet for your senses to make your husband love you even more than when he was the suitor! Look out! in battling with your husband you say you fight Conscience; with Mademoiselle Daniels, with whom I have had twenty minutes' pleasant conversation, enlightening him, you would conflict with Virtue. Tell your husband that the money you offered to help him, came out of our bank, and he will not forgive you or tolerate you this time. No, for his silence would no longer be loftiness of soul, but complicity of which I do not think him capable," he grudgingly said. "He would hand you over to the police, and believe me, the Emperor Napoleon, having a mania on the subject of artillery, would personally instruct his *procureur* to draw up an indictment against you which would not miss fire. And were you to escape in France, we should have that abstracted money's worth from you elsewhere. Now, dear lady, for how much will you sell us the secret of M. Clemenceau?"

The woman bowed her head, like one imprisoned in a sand drift, not to be crossed in any direction, but closing in and weighing down. She was in a pitfall, overpowered like Gratian had been, subjugated, soon to be put to the yoke and compelled to draw steadily the harrow of transcendental politics. Her caprices, faults, fancies, duplicities, wiles, caresses, impudence, conquests and delights were but straws out of which some great diplomatist would draw supplies for his cattle. It was humiliating to the superb creature, but logical. She gnashed her teeth, but she was sure that her cajolery—even her tears would be thrown away on this soldier-spy whom once she had jilted, and who at present surfeited himself with her defeat.

"It is a crime," she moaned, "a dastardly crime that you require me to do."

"Not your first! You robbed us for your own private ends—we want you to rob another for ours! you must not always be selfish."

"But I had really repented—"

"Pooh! you may repent of this fresh misdeed while you are about penance. I have no objections to you becoming a good wife! it will be a novel sensation, and of nothing are you more fond! Suppose you convince your husband that it is wicked to kill his fellow-men by the myriad—that love of woman is better than glory—decide him to go into a cottage by the Mediterranean with you, and—sell us the invention. We could put it to a righteous end; clear Africa of cannibals, that the merchants' stores, and farms to raise produce to fill them, should replace cane-huts. But I doubt you will succeed!"

"Never!" she exclaimed, afraid that her hopelessness would injure her, for she would be the creditor of this remorseless combination without any prospect of repaying them. But all resistance was useless, she was convinced; she had to submit or she would be expunged from life. She who had fancied herself so powerful was but the lowly, abject subaltern at the beck of a preponderating power of which she understood no more the details than the aim and principle.

"There is always a second course," observed Von Sendlingen slowly. "That weak, inexperienced, young Italian, who loves you passionately."

"Antonino?"

"Antonino, yes; he carries the key to that coffer, and the key, too, of the private cipher in which the inventor records his discoveries."

Shrinking away aghast, her blanched countenance expressed her wonder at this preternatural knowledge. These master-spies knew everything, even under this roof, better than the wife! This grim giant carried on an abominable craft with thorough insight. That she could never emulate, for completeness was not her forte. Oh, had she but been a virtuous woman—an honorable wife, he had not dared assume to govern her! but when of a girl's age, she had acted like a woman; when a wife she had acted like the dissolute and unwived; when a mother, she had disembarrassed herself of the token of her glory of maternity. She was not fit to be anything but the instrument of such universal conspirators. She whom the viscount had playfully called "Donna Juana!" had met the Statue of the Commander at last, and once grasped, she would no more be free.

"I shall report to our committee that we have made our agreement," he said calmly and then, as he proceeded toward the door with the jolly swagger of the Marseillais transforming his stalwart and rigid frame, he added in the southern bland tone, "Delighted to see you again, dear Madame Clemenceau!"

She did not hear him, for she had sunk too deeply within the abyss. She regretted she had come back. It is true that the company which he represented so terrifyingly, might have pursued her and pestered her for their money, but she had the gifts that would arouse defenders for her in any quarter of the globe.

Had she not one ally? certainly no friend! and yet, if Clemenceau would only help her a little, she might cope with the arch-intriguer. If, indeed, Felix did not save her, she would be lost. It was a dreadful game, but glorious to win it, and she would be another and worthy woman if she came out unwounded. In her distress, she would have had recourse to the Jew and have utilized Rebecca though her rival, too! Besides, there was Antonino, so passionate as to rush blindly, dagger in hand, on even a Von Sendlingen.

"Come, come, cheer up," she said to herself, "there is a chance or two yet. If only I could get over this crisis, I will reform and sincerely resolve not to do a single act for which to reproach myself!"

XVIII

A Bitter Parting

With a somewhat less burdened mind, Césarine was still pondering when she saw Antonino, who had opened the door but perceived her, about to withdraw without notifying her of his presence. It was the act of a devotee who feared to pray in the chapel, when the priestess stood by the saint's image.

"Do not go," she exclaimed with vehemence. "Come here after closing the door tightly, for I want you to enter into a little plot with me."

She had regained her smiling visage and her sweet voice.

"Would you do it?"

"It depends upon who the object is," he said tremulously.

"It is against my husband," she replied with her smile more bright and her tone more merry.

"I forewarn you, madame, that I should turn informer," he answered in the same light key, but forced.

"That would be very bad for him for I am conspiring for his benefit."

"In that case, madame, I am entirely your man."

"Are you able to keep a secret?" she asked with gravity.

"I think so."

They had withdrawn into the window recess, and could see the gardens, as they conversed. The light fell on her through the Valenciennes curtain and at her back was a sombre tapestry. Her late trial gave her an exhausted air which seemed the additional gloss with which melancholy makes a woman more fascinating in the sentimental eyes of youth.

"I dare say you can keep your own," she pointedly said.

"Not so well, I fear, as another's."

"You must give me your word of honor that if my plot does not please you, nobody shall be told?"

"I give you my promise," he said freely, just as he would have given her anything she asked for.

He had debated with his passion, uttered every reason of others and all he could devise, overwhelmed himself with good advice and created a Chinese Wall of obstacles, but he heard himself murmuring: "I love her!" The only way, he feared, to put an end to his wicked craze was to put an end to his life—an irreputable argument, but to be used moderately. She allowed him to quiver under her lingering gaze, and finally said:

"The fact is, I do not like the idea of M. Clemenceau selling this house. It would be a greater grief than he believes now. He has his dearest memories springing here. Besides, he could not work in peace in town. Fortunately, my uncle has provided me with the means to help him. I want to lend him the sum required, but I fear that he would accept nothing from me."

"He is a very proud man," observed the Italian, courteously, for, while he worshiped the speaker, he knew that she was not morally without blemishes.

Not because her affection for him was a proof of that delinquency, for love overlooked that and gave it another name, but because he believed Clemenceau, and the woman, while no less alluring, was terrifying as well.

"It is an excess of very cruel justice!" said she with a strange warmth. "The greatest punishment on a wrongdoer is to refuse her, when repentant, the joy of doing a kindness. You need not pretend surprise, for I have done harm. I did not forsee what would be thought of my hasty conduct, and even if I were wicked; can you expect a woman to have the loftiness of genius like him, and the force for resisting temptation like you?"

"Like me!" exclaimed Antonino, starting.

"Yes; can you deny that you have had to wrestle and are wrestling now with yourself most strenuously?"

He averted his eyes and made no reply.

"Child that you are," she resumed. "You were right when you just now said that you could keep the secret of others better than your own. Can the eyes of an honest youth like you deceive those of a wayward woman like me? I thank you for the effort you have made—and the silence your lips have preserved. It matters not. I am glad that after doing the act of reparation proposed, I shall have the means to go away, literally, for good this time. It is time I went."

He lifted his hand as if to detain her, but let it fall quickly.

After all, if she departed forever without speaking out the secret of those two hearts, what harm would be done. Who had the right to prevent the susceptible Italian feeling the first impressions of the gentler sex and owing them to Césarine? He could but be thankful that he saw only the prologue to "the great dreadful tragedy of Woman." He might blame himself for cherishing the memory of the false wife, but he could not annul that early sensation. Was it her fault, brought to France at the sequel of a romantic adventure, if she met him, a castaway, and disturbed his youth and innocence? There had not seemed any evil intention in speech or behavior toward him, and he himself might be as proud as she was of the pure and respectful sentiment which should have contributed toward her amelioration. In this case, he—ignorant of the counter-attraction of the Viscount de Terremonde—imagined that she had struggled also against the pressure of nature and the sin was no more when she triumphed.

"Well, listen to the secret which we can discuss," said she. "I wish to be associated with you in a good action, which, I hope, will lead to many another, if it is the first. One of these days, when you learn the story of my life, you will see there was a little good in it to shine on the dark background. Are you not willing to help me increase it? In this case, that good and honorable man will profit."

Antonino listened spellbound, he could have been ordered up to their own terrible cannon's mouth by that resistless voice.

"Let me live one day in your youth, illusions and unstained conscience," she implored. "Well, here in this little pocketbook are letters of credit for two hundred thousand francs. It is all I have—take it."

"What am I to do with it?" said Antonino.

"Put it away somewhere out of my reach to retake it. I know myself and that, if I have a good thought one day, I might entertain the reverse on the next. If I broke into the money, I could not replace the sum extracted, and, another thing, I cannot make the use of it I intended. Leave me to win from my husband the acceptance of the help I wish to give him. It may take long, but until then, pray keep the money; that will not entangle you in any degree."

What a strange woman! he thought. She does evil with the easy, graceful air of an almsgiver distributing charity, and she does good with the stealth of a criminal!

"I am a fair example of my sex," said she, divining what was in his mind, "weak, ignorant, unfortunate: and stupid—and the proof is any harm I have done to others is nothing to that I have wrought to myself."

Antonino, taking the pocketbook—a dainty article in Russian leather—went to the oaken chest which he opened after what seemed some cabalistic manipulation, and the muttering of what seemed an "Open Sesame!"

"Have you no safe yet, is that box strong and secure?" she inquired in a tone of well assumed anxiety, as she hurriedly took three or four steps to bring her again beside him.

"You need not be alarmed. That is a box of which we made the peculiar fastenings. It is too heavy to be carried off, and burglars will not tamper with it in impunity," said the Italian, smiling maliciously, as he put his hand on the lid to raise it.

"I understand; it opens with a secret lock?"

"Yes; one I cannot tell you about."

"I have no use for it," she said hastily, "on the contrary, I wish the money to be where I cannot touch it."

"Nobody will touch it there," returned the young man gravely. "Stop! how will you get it if anything happens to me—if I should die?"

"A young man like you die in a couple of days!" laughed Césarine.

"It may occur," he replied gloomily. "Death has hovered over this house at any moment of some of our experiments with the most powerful essences of nature. And only this morning, when I was out to the post-office, they were talking of a hideous discovery—a young man's remains, found in a ditch in the Five Hectare Field."

"A—a young man?"

"A foreigner, some said; but his clothes were in tatters, and the water-rats had disfigured him."

"Poor fellow!" said she, and quickly she added as if eager to change the subject: "my name is on the letters of credit. In case of any mishap, I will plainly say so to my husband and he will return me my own property."

That was sensible. He had no farther remonstrances to offer, and taking advantage of her glancing out into the garden, he closed the lid and fastened it so that she could not see how the trick was done. She was not vexed, for she saw that man is always weak and on the point of losing his Paradise. Antonino would betray as the price of love. She allowed him to go in to luncheon alone, wishing to inspect the mysterious casket; but, unluckily, she was interrupted by Hedwig, who rather officiously wanted to dust the room. Not for the first time, Césarine, remembering the wide occult sway claimed by Colonel Von

Sendlingen, suspected that the girl was not so much her ally as she wished. She had begun to watch her under the impression that she was in confederacy with Mademoiselle Daniels. She had perceived no signs of that, but she believed she intercepted an exchange of glances with the false Marseillais. They were of the same nationality and this fact caused Césarine to be on her guard. Unless Hedwig repeated what had happened between Clemenceau and Antonino, how could the colonel know of their conversation?

Hesitating to question her directly, disliking her from that moment, and feeling her heart shrink at her loneliness when such crushing odds were threatening her, she donned her "company smile" and went to the sitting-room bravely.

XIX

The Compact

Luncheon was served and M. Cantagnac, seated comfortably, was trying the delicacies with rare conscientiousness about any escaping his harpoon-like fork. Césarine did not give him a second look and neither he nor Clemenceau, with whom he was chatting on politics, more than glanced up at her. M. Daniels was more polite, for he warmly accepted a second cup of coffee as soon as she, without any attempt to displace Mademoiselle Daniels at the urn, took her place beside her.

"Pray go on and attend to the liquors," she said kindly. "I am so nervous that I am afraid I shall break something."

She took a seat which placed her on the left of the old Jew. A little familiarity was only in keeping when two theatrical artists met.

"What is the matter with your daughter? she seems sad," she remarked with apparent interest.

"That is natural enough when we are going away from France, it may be forever."

"Going away from here?" inquired Madame Clemenceau.

"Yes; this evening, but we did not like to go without bidding you good-bye. Now that we have seen you in good health, and thanked you for your hospitality, we can proceed on our mission without compunction."

"A mission—where?"

"I have succeeded in interesting capitalists in your husband's inventions. That is settled; and I have taken up again a holy undertaking which should hardly have been laid aside for a mere money matter. But there is nothing more sacred, after all, than friendship, I owe to your husband more than I have thus far repaid," and he bent a tender regard on his daughter, with its overflow upon Clemenceau one of gratitude.

"Are you going far?" asked Césarine, keeping her eyes in play but little rewarded by her scrutiny of the sham Marseillais who devoured, like an old campaigner, never sure of the next meal, or of Rebecca who superintended the table in her stead with a serious unconcern.

"Around the world," replied Daniels simply, "straight on to the East."

"Goodness! it is folly to take a young lady with you. Is it a scientific errand? No, you said holy. Religious?"

"Scientific of an exalted type."

"Is science somewhat entertaining for young ladies?"

"Some think it so."

"She might not. Leave her with me. We are comrades of art, you know," smiling up cordially at Rebecca, as if they had been friends of childhood and had never parted any more than Venus' coupled loves.

"Where?"

"In our house," Césarine replied, as though she were fully assured that the smiling man on the opposite side of the board would not obtain the property. "I do not think we shall quit it."

"If she likes," answered Daniels, easily.

"Rebecca!" he gently called, "Madame invites you to stay with her during my journey. M. Clemenceau is my dearest friend, and from the time of his wife consenting, do not constrain yourself into going if you would rather remain."

"I thank you, madame," replied the Jewess, "but I am going with my father, because we have never quitted one another, and I do not wish to leave him alone."

"Dear child!" exclaimed Daniels embracing her before he let her return to the head of the table. "She will not listen to any suggestion of marriage. I know of a bright young gentleman who adores her—an Israelite like us, in a promising position. He will one day be a professor at the Natural History Museum. But she would not hear of him."

"It is not very amusing to live among birds, beasts and reptiles," said Césarine.

"Ha, ha! but then those are stuffed," exclaimed her opposite neighbor, showing that he was listening.

"Very likely, she cherishes some little fancy in her heart," said Madame Clemenceau, thinking of both her husband and Antonino.

"Possibly," said the Jew, complacently, for he knew that his daughter was very fair.

"I believe I know the object," continued Madame Clemenceau.

"I am rather astonished that she should have told you, and not me."

"Oh, she has not told me anything, I guessed."

Daniels seemed relieved.

"And if you should like to hear the name," she began rapidly, but he stopped her with a dignified smile. "What, you do not want to know what I have found before you, and so much concerns you!"

"If she has not told me, it is because she does not want me to know," he observed placidly.

"But what if she tells him!" persisted Césarine.

"She would not let her lover know the state of her heart without informing her father; she would commence with me."

The wife smiled cynically at such unlimited trust and felt her hatred of Rebecca augment.

"There are not many fathers like you!"

"Nor many daughters like her," he retorted proudly. "I am of the opinion that there is a mistake in the French mode of educating girls. The truth about everything should be told them, as is done to their brothers. The ignorance in which they are left often arises from their parents themselves not knowing the causes and end of things, or have no time, or have lost the right to speak of everything to their children from their own errors or passions. My wife was the best of women and I believe Rebecca takes after her. When she was of the age of comprehension, I began to explain the world to her simply and clearly. All of heaven's work is noble; no human soul—even a virgin's—has the right to be shocked by any feature of it. Rebecca aided me when I sought to make a livelihood by the profession of music, to which she had strong proclivities."

Clemenceau was listening in courtesy to this argument, and the false Marseillais did not lose a word—or a sip of his Kirschwasser.

"Afterward, when my ideas changed, and I could make my way to fortune by a thoroughfare, less under the public eye, I associated her in my studies. She knows," proceeded Daniels, who had shaken off a spell of taciturnity which the stranger and Madame Clemenceau had inspired, and seemed unable to pause, "she knows that nothing can be destroyed, and that all undergoes transformation, and cannot cease to exists with the exception of evil which diminishes as it goes on its way."

Cantagnac slowly absorbed another glass of the cherry cordial, which he had to pour out himself as Rebecca had retired to a corner where the host turned over the leaves of photographic album as a cover to their dialogue.

"If my daughter loves," continued Daniels, seeing at last that his theme was too abstruse for his single auditor, "as you conjectured, dear madame, it is surely some honorable person worthy of that love; if she has not informed me it is because there is some obstacle, such as the man's not loving her or being bound to another woman. In any case, the obstacle must be insurmountable, or she would not go away with me into strange countries through great fatigue on a chimerical search."

Cantagnac had risen and, very courteously for his assumed character, had come round the table without going near his host and the Jewess, and entered into the other dialogue.

"Did you say you were going far, monsieur?" he inquired.

Daniels nodded and opened his arms significantly to their utmost extent.

"Leaving Europe with a scientific design? Ah! may one hear?"

"Perhaps it would not much interest you?" returned the old man, who seemed to feel a revival of a prejudice against the visitor upon his coming nearer.

"The atmosphere of this house is so learned," replied, the smiling man unabashed by the sudden coolness, "and, besides, more things interest me than people believe, eh, madame?" directly appealing to the hostess, who had to nod.

"You see I have a great deal of spare time since I retired from business and I am eager to increase my store, ha, ha!"

"Well, the idea which has tormented more than one of my race, has seized me," returned M. Daniels, "I wish to fill up gaps in our traditional story and link our present and our future with our past. The question is of the Lost Tribes of Israel. I believe after some research, that I know the truth on the subject, and, more that I may be chosen to reconquer our country. The ideal one is not sufficient for us, and I am going to locate the real one and register the act of claiming it. Every man has his craze or his ideal, and mine may lead me from China to Great Salt Lake, or to the Sahara."

"What a pity," interjected Cantagnac merrily, "that the Wandering Jew did not have your idea. It would have helped him work out his sentence to walk around the globe!"

"He had no money to lend to monarchs sure to vanquish or to peoples astounded by having been overcome. But his five pence have fructified by dint of much patience, privation and economy. The Wandering Jew has realized the legend and ceases to tramp. He has reached the goal. What do you think about my pleasure tour?" he suddenly inquired of Clemenceau, whose eye he caught. "Child of Europe, happy son of Japhet. I am going to see old Shem and Ham. Have you a keepsake to send them or a promise to make?"

"Tell them," said the host, coming over to join the group, while Rebecca, during the continued resignation of Madame Clemenceau, superintended the servant's removal of the luncheon service, "tell them that we are all hard at work here and that more than ever there's a chance of our becoming one family."

On seeing Clemenceau approach his wife, the pretended Marseillais delicately withdrew to the corner of the sideboard where the cigar-stand tempted him. But he kept his eyes secretly on the two men who gave him more concern than the two women. He reflected that fate had managed things wisely for his plans, for if Clemenceau had married the incorruptible Jewess, he might have been more surely foiled. As for Daniels, the amateur apostle who hinted at a union of his people, he might be dangerous or useful. He determined to put a spy on his track, who might smear his face with ochre and stick an eagle's feather in his cap so that, if seen to shoot him in a New Mexican canon, that supposed lost Tribe of Israel which include the Apaches would gain the credit of the murder. While reflecting, his quick ear heard a light loot draw near; he did not look round, sure that it was his new recruit who crept up to him. It was, indeed, Madame Clemenceau, who put his half-emptied liquor glass upon the sideboard by him.

"No heeltapi in our house, Monsieur!" she exclaimed.

Cantagnac tossed off the concentrated cordial with contempt; his head was not one to be affected by such potations.

"Thank you! have you already opened the trenches?" he asked in an undertone.

"By means of the Italian, yes. I have entered the stronghold."

"But he closed the door in your face!"

"No, no; I can open it at any time."

"Excellent Kisschwasser, this of yours, madame!" exclaimed Von Sendlingen, in his satisfaction speaking the word with a little too accurate a pronunciation to suit a native of the south of France.

"Mark that man!" whispered Rebecca to Clemenceau, whom she had rejoined as he stood by her father. "Distrust him! his laugh is forced and false! I am sure that he wishes you evil!"

"Then stay here and shield the house!"

"No; I must go this evening. Ah, you men of brains laugh at us women for entertaining presentiments. But we do have them and we must utter them. Be on your guard!"

"And must you go?" went on Clemenceau to Daniels, as if he expected to find him less resolute than his daughter.

"More than ever!" but, seeing how he had saddened him, he took his hand with much emotion and added: "Rebecca will explain. I go away happy to think that the honest men outnumber the other sort and that when we all take hold of hands, we shall see that the scoundrels excluded from our ring will be scarcely worth disabling from farther injury."

Césarine, perceiving that her confederate was edging gradually toward the rifle which Antonino had been shooting with and which had been removed from the drawing-room, where the guest for a day had too many opportunities to be alone with it. To cover his inspection, she suggested that Rebecca should afford the company a final pleasure, a kind of swan's song, and went and opened the cottage-piano for her. The Jewess did not refuse the invitation and began Gounod's "Medje" in a voice which Von Sendlingen had room to admit had improved in tone and volumn, and would make her as worthy of the grand opera house as it had, five years before, of the Harmonista and its class. Daniels quietly left the room, loth to disturb Clemenceau, whom that voice enthralled and who became more and more deeply submerged in the thoughts it engendered. He suffered pain from the need to liberate his sorrows, confide his spirit and communicate his dreams. And was not this singer the very one created to comfort him and lull him to rest? Must he remain heroic and ridiculous in the indissoluble bond, and endure silently. On Antonino he rested his mind and on Rebecca, the daughter of the eternally persecuted, he longed to rest his soul.

The greatness of this man and the purity of this gifted creature were so clearly made for one another that everybody divined and understood the unspoken, immaterial love.

What an oversight to have let Césarine abduct him when it was Rebecca to whom chance had shown that he ought to belong! If he had remained free till this second meeting, she would have been his wife, his companion his seventh day repose, and the mother of his earthly offspring instead of the immortal twins, genius and glory, which poorly consoled the childless husband! As it was, the powers constituted would not allow them to dwell near each other. She could only be the bride in the second life—for eternity. She loved him as few women had ever loved, because he was good, great and just—and because he was unhappy. No man existed in her eyes superior to him.

Nothing but death would set him free from the woman who had not appreciated him properly. She had let pass the greatest bliss a woman can know on earth—the love of a true heart and the protection of a great intellect. If death struck them before the wife, Felix would behold Rebecca on the threshold of the unknown land where they would be united tor infinity. Her creed did not warrant such a hope—his said that in heaven there were no marriages, but her heart did not heed such sayings, and her feelings told her that thus things would come to pass.

She had concluded the piece of music. She rose and, for the first time, gave Césarine her hand.

"Farewell!" she said.

"Why say it now?" answered Madame Clemenceau, surprised. "You are not going till to-morrow morning."

"To-night! I may not see you again, we have so many preparations to make."

"Well, as you did not come here to see me, it is of no consequence. Farewell!"

"I am your servant, madame," said the Jewess, bowing.

"Ah, Hagar!" hissed she, "unmasked."

"Farewell, Sarah!" retorted Rebecca, stung out of her equanimity by this sudden dart of the viper, but Césarine said no more, and she proceeded steadily toward the door.

Clemenceau had preceded her thither.

"What did she say?" he inquired.

"Nothing worth repeating. Beware of her as well as of that man!" but she saw that he would not follow her glance and draw a serious inference from the way in which the wife and the unwelcome guest had drawn closely together. "Fulfil your destiny," she continued solemnly. "Work! remain firm, pure and great! Be useful to mankind. Above transient things, in the unalterable, I will await you. Do not keep me lonely too long," was wrung from her in a doleful sob.

He could not speak, it was useless, for she knew already everything that he night say.

"At last!" exclaimed Von Sendlingen in relief, when all had gone out, as he sprang on the rifle and feverishly fingered it. "This is the rifle of their latest finish. What an odd arrangement! Where the deuce is the hammer—the trigger—and all that goes toward making up the good old rifle of our fathers? Oh, Science, Science! what liberties are taken in your name!" he cried in drollery too bitter not to be intended to cover his vexation. "Mind, this rifle is included in our contract?"

"Everything," she answered in a fever, looking toward the doorway, where her husband had disappeared with the Jewess. "Be easy! The rifle, the cannon, the happiness, the honor and the lives of all here—myself as well! If there is anything more you long for, say so!"

"Talk sensibly!" said he severely and gripping her wrist.

Restored by the pressure, she drew a long breath and said in a low voice:

"One way or another, things will come to a head to-night. This Jewish intriguante and the old fox her father are going away by the railway at nine o'clock, and Felix will escort them. Antonino will be alone here, and I mean to make him my assistant as he has been my husband's."

"Better trust nobody! it is risky, and, besides, with an accomplice, the reward becomes less by his share."

"How much is all? Will you pay five million marks?"

"That's too much. Put it two millions—half when you hand over the cipher, half when we hold the working drawings and Antonino's ammunition."

"Be it so," she answered after a brief pause, during which both listened. "If Antonino will help me, so much the better for him. It would be delightful to see Italy with a native! Now go away. We must not be seen conversing together."

"If the young man turns restive?" suggested the prudent spy.

"Impossible! he is charmed. However, remember this: Return to-night after the party has gone to the station, secrete yourself in the grounds where you can watch the drawing-room windows. If one opens and I call, run up to aid me. If none open to you, hasten away. The danger with which I contend will be one which you could not overcome!"

XX

On the Eve

The evening was calm and clear over Montmorency, where there was even grandeur in the stillness. Nature—the discreet confident and inexhaustible counsellor, always ready to intermediate between God and man—nature was appeasing passion and misery in all bosoms but Felix Clemenceau's, as he strolled in the garden which he did not expect long to possess. Rebecca was going away and Césarine had come, two sufficient reasons for him to detest the place. He had called upon the scene to give him advice on his course, and he hoped to understand clearly what it had commanded to him in the hour of grief tempered with faith. He had not the resources of others; he could not consult the shades of his parents; his mother's tomb was not one to be pointed out with pride, any more than his father's.

It seemed to him that he was ordered to continue struggling till he vanquished; this he had always tried. Work and seek out! And yet his mind wavered and his resolve was unsettled. It was the ever dulcet voice of that Circe which sufficed to agitate and obscure his soul in spite of his having believed it was forever detached from her. But these umbrageous and odoriferous hills, knew how deeply he loved her, for he had spoken of his thraldom to them when he might not speak to her under pain of shame and debasement.

Had he not undergone enough and pardoned as far as could be expected? But she had disdained condonation, mocked at it and trampled it under foot.

Again she came to entangle him in her love. No; her wiles and witchery, for she was not a woman to love anyone or anything. Unable to love her own flesh and blood, she was an alien to humanity, as well as to love. To such a mother, he owed solely indifference.

Such a woman was only a human form, less to him than the least of the patient, laborious animals useful to man.

As the stars grew darkened by clouds above the impassible horizon, his reflections turned more gloomy and deadly. Was it impious for him to arrogate the right to substitute his justice for that supreme, and wield its dreadful sword? But he shrank from acting as his father had done, and mainly because he saw that, if ever the world knew that he loved Rebecca, it would say that he had slain his wife to clear the path to the altar for his second marriage.

Césarine had hinted of repentance, her return portended the same. The world would side with her. Yes; he would give her another chance. After the guests departed, he would let Antonino also go, he would resign himself to being coupled again with this chain-companion in the galleys of life!

"If it is true," he concluded, "I will endeavor to lead her to the light and truth, although her soul is full of shadows and the divine spark is clogged with ashes. Oh, heaven, may she be filled with the temptation to do good and mayest thou receive her in thy endless mercifulness!"

The squeaking of the gravel under a regular and heavy step induced him to look round, and a burly shape loomed up in the darkness between the plane trees. It was the so-called Cantagnac, who bowed, with his hat off.

"I have been hunting for you everywhere," he said jovially. "I want to say good-bye without company by, for it makes me timid, ha, ha! though you would not think it. Nice wholesome air, here! cool, decidedly cool, but wholesome. Doing a solitary smoke over a new invention?"

"No, monsieur, I was conversing."

"Eh! but I do not see anybody!"

"I was conversing with Nature."

"Oh, what the poet-fellows call musing, eh?"

"A kind of prayer."

"I see! well, his church is always open and you can go to service anytime, and day or night! and no collection-plate, ha, ha!"

"I make it a practice every day, if only briefly."

"Quite right! quite! I am inclined that way myself, since I lost my wife and our boy. He said something about hoping to meet me one day up there!" and he flourished his handkerchief about his eyes and toward the clouds. "Blessed relief to pray and do you really get an answer now and then? in time, no doubt, for it's a great way off!"

"Do you not believe in heaven, M. Cantagnac?" demanded Clemenceau, bluntly.

In the twilight and loneliness, the question struck home, and the spy felt compelled to make some answer.

"My dear M. Clemenceau," he faltered, "I never meddle with matters which do not teach me anything. One word has existed thousands of years, and yet full explanations on the highest secrets have been wholly refused, so that the finest intellects give up seeking them unless they want to go mad. So I think it my duty to abstain and not lose my time in studies useless and dangerous. It is not merely a matter of reasoning, but of prudence. Of course, every man is his own master. I grant that we certainly are subjected to a power above our wit and will. We are born without knowing how, and die without knowing why. Between birth and death, swarm struggles, passions, sorrows, maladies, miseries of all kinds; an unfair, uneven sharing of worldly goods, and scoundrels often happy and triumphant and honest people most often unhappy and erroneously judged. We are told that we should adore and praise this state of things; but I only hold such events as certainties that I can see and turn to my profitable use. Now you, M. Clemenceau, are a honorable man—a great man since you can carry on a conversation with Nature! Why not ask her a favor on account of your belief and your work? so that you will not have to doubt her some day more than I do. But let us talk of more substantial things. I have inspected the plan of the property and walked over the grounds. I have your agent's address, and in a week, I will write to him and make my offer. I dare say we shall come to an agreement. Let me thank you for your very kind welcome—I shall be off in ten minutes."

Absorbed in meditation, Clemenceau did not hold out his hand, and, with the idea upon him of the engagement with Madame Clemenceau, the spy did not remind him of the omission.

"You need not walk over to the station, for M. Daniels and his daughter are going in my carriage. I will find you a place."

This arrangement might have necessitated the false Marseillais going into the cars and getting out at the next station; so he excused himself on the plea that the walk would please him better.

"To tell you the truth, I am bound to take exercise or die of apoplexy—so my family doctor tells me. By the way, I have taken leave already of Madame Clemenceau. A Russian, you tell me? I never should have imagined it! Ah, one can see that you have converted her into a true French lady—lucky man! I can understand that you believe in lofty ideas beside a beautiful and talented woman like her! Lucky, lucky man!"

And he turned aside, calling out as he departed:

"I know my way! give my respects to your friends who are hunting for the Lost Tribes! ha, ha!"

This laugh, loud but not jolly as it was intended to appear, routed Clemenceau's solemn thoughts. It seemed, like Pan's, from a statue, which gleamed in a vista, still to reverberate when the inventor went back to the house. At the upper windows gleamed lights which moved to and fro, and shadows flitted across the openings; it was the usual bustle when guests are packing up, and the idea of the too quiet and lonely house, of the morrow saddens the observer.

A woman's form darted across the lawn and made the master start. It came along easily, and he saw that it was one familiar with the grounds.

"Hedwig!"

It was the servant who had run out to the stables to see that the horses were put to the carriage.

"Stop a minute! we are in privacy here, and I want to have a word with you."

The girl paused, intimidated and almost frightened; she lost color as she stood, agitatedly, shifting her weight from one foot to the other, and averting her eyes from the speaker. A thief caught in a felonious act would not have presented a more damning spectacle.

"Not only are we breaking up the household, Hedwig, but the house is going to other hands. The mistress and I will live in a hotel at Paris for some time, on account of my changed business relations. Consequently, we must dispense with your services. Madame will, on grand occasions, have a professional hair dresser in, and so—in a word, I must ask you to please yourself about returning to your own country, or seeking another situation in this one. You can refer to Madame for a character; for, I believe, you have always served her faithfully. But you need not look to her for a present, too. Here is a couple of hundred franc notes by way of notice. I wish you well wherever you go."

To the amazement of the speaker, instead of accepting the token of kindness, Hedwig suddenly put both hands behind her back, and stood confounded. Tears silently flowed down her cheeks; then, falling on her knees, she sobbed:

"Oh, master, I do not deserve this! Oh, master please forgive me! I am a very wicked girl!"

"What are you about?" he exclaimed, fearing that the unexpected boon had crazed her. "Do get up!"

"No, no; not before master forgives me!" moaned she.

"Oh, yes, yes—anything!" aiding her to rise.

But she continued weeping, and with the fluency in the illiterate when they have long brooded over a speech to relieve their mind, she said:

"You don't know what goes on, master! but I am forced to tell you now, since you are so good. I have always been in madame's service since we came out of Germany. I was devoted to her, and I knew her when I was at the Persepolitan Hotel, but devotion when women are concerned, becomes complicity.

"Madame never has cared for you, monsieur, for you and yours. She did not marry you for any liking, but because of spite. Not spite from your father having punished one of her precious family—they are all a bad lot—a witch's brood! faugh! but to Mademoiselle Daniels whom she feared would secure the prize. Madame carried on dreadful! When she went away last time, it is true she had a telegram from her uncle—but that was a happy accident. She was going to bolt anyway, and that came in so nicely! She was planning to elope with one of her conquests—the Viscount—"

"I know!"

"You know? Well, you don't know that the dead man found in the ditch was the Viscount—"

"I saw him killed!" in the same measured tone.

"Oh!" She paused, but recovering, she continued, in a lower voice and looking furtively around: "You cannot know that she came back with no good end. I believe it was to meet the gentleman who came in at the same time, a-pretending to buy the house—"

"M. Cantagnac!" muttered the inventor, a tolerable flock of suspicions which that ingenious individual had unintentionally excited, rushing upon his brain.

"He's no Marseillais—he's a German, and he is a secret agent. He is—he is—well, I may make a clean breast of it—he is one you ought to have remembered, the major whom you cudgelled in Munich—"

"Von Sendlingen!"

"Yes, and a colonel—I do not know but he is a general now; he has the manner and means of one!" said Hedwig, shuddering. "He knows all of madame's peccadilloes—ay, all her crimes—"

"Crimes! be careful, girl!"

"Yes, crime, for she killed her little boy! Thank heaven, I had no hand in that—she would not trust me there, and that shows I am not so very bad a woman, don't it? She poisoned the little innocent as surely as we stand here under the eye of God!"

"Go on; go on," said Clemenceau, hoarsely.

"The colonel threatened to tell you these and other things unless she consented to sell him all your business secrets—and give him the model gun that goes off without any powder and caps."

"Ah! she consented?" growled the inventor, grinding his teeth and his eyes kindling.

"Nobody can hold out against the colonel. He soon made me play the spy on everybody for his benefit. But this is not all!"

"Not all! what a sink of iniquity! Would she poison Mademoiselle Rebecca, too?"

"I do not doubt it! The old witch her grandmother must have taught her all the tricks of her trade. But I meant to say that she is setting her cap at poor, dear, young M. Antonino—"

"I know that. Take your money! and live honestly."

"No, monsieur," she replied with some dignity. "And here is money that the colonel gave me. It burns me! I beg you to give it toward some good work, which you understand better than me. Will you not—and forgive me?"

"Have you anything more to say?"

"I have been peeping and listening, but they are all very cunning. I only gleaned that the colonel who has just gone out as if to the station, should return later and hang around to have the rifle and some papers delivered to him."

"By Antonino?"

"If your wife can make him a cat's-paw; if not, she is capable of doing all herself—though, anyway, she is driven to it. But, monsieur, it burdened me and if you had not called me, I was coming to tell you of their schemes. I do not like your idea of killing people by hundreds, but it may be good to honest folks, beset by savages and such like, and it is not right of a servant to let a master be robbed by more than bandits and brigands."

"I am grateful to you, girl." She seized his hand and covered it with grateful kisses. "Keep your money and this I give you. Do good with your own hand, then it will bless both giver and receiver, as is written."

"Monsieur, you are too good. Could I ask a favor—a proof that you do not think me altogether bad? Will you recommend me to Mademoiselle Daniels. The Jews do not object to Christian servants, and, besides," she said with simplicity, "I am so poor a Christian."

"You shall enter her service. You will continue, reformed under her charge. Go and pack up and hasten from this house—accursed as an eyrie of vultures!"

"I am glad you have the warning. Excuse me, but if you were to do like the colonel only pretend to go away and come back here to use your ears and eyes, you would see what happens."

By the look that passed over her master's face, the girl, though no wise woman, perceived that she had mistaken. He was not the sort to act like a Von Sendlingen and hide himself to peep and listen. He would be no better than herself if he acted thus.

"I have advised you to go away with the Daniels. I shall drive the party over in the carriage to the station and return as though I knew of nothing. There are times for men to act; times for God to have a clear field. Persevere in the right path, girl, and say no more to anybody not even Mademoiselle Daniels."

"But you will be seeing madame first?" inquired the girl, fearing the collision to which she had contributed, but lighter of soul since she had flashed the danger-signal.

"M. Antonino first, and then your mistress," replied he in a stern tone which put an end to the dialogue.

XXI

The Last Appeal

I n the large room where Césarine was to achieve her crowning act of treachery, she and her husband were closeted. On the latter's unruffled brow not even her feline gaze could read what a perfect acquaintance he possessed with all her past and her purposed moves.

"Your maid tells me that you wished to speak to me," he said.

"It is necessary, on the eve of a change in our mode of life, so extreme as a home broken up in favor of a stay at a hotel."

"I am listening to you," he said curtly.

"If I were to say to you that I love you, what would be your answer?" she said, changing the subject and her tone entirely.

"Nothing! I might wonder what new evil you intended to commit to my prejudice. Pure curiosity for you can do nothing more with me."

She was convinced of that, and she thrilled with all the irritation of a woman who has lost her power of fascination over even one man.

"Admitting that I cannot do you any harm," she said, "others may and, perhaps a great deal. Would you believe that I love you at least if my pledge of love consisted in my aiding you to repel the harm and to triumph over your enemies at the risk of the greatest danger to myself?"

He shook his head resolutely.

"What other proof do you want?"

He intimated that he could do without any aid from her.

"I am sincere, I swear it!" she exclaimed.

"On what can you swear?"

"It would appear that you, whom people rate as a saint, and so just, do not believe in repentance?"

"I do!"

"Then, I repent," said she, rolling her eyes like Magdalen in a Guido picture.

"No; those repenting do not say so before they prove it—they give the evidence and do not boast."

"But what if I have no time to wait?" she said piteously. "What if it is necessary for my soul's sake and perhaps for yours, that I should tell you at once what I intended to exhibit gradually when I arrived? make the effort to believe me without delay, for one single minute may redeem my blackened life and save all to come. Is it so hard for you to listen to me, and to believe me?" she wailed. "It would only be renewing an old habit of yours, for you used to love me, and ardently, too! The first kiss you ever gave to a woman, and the only ones you ever received from a woman, are mine! you see I do not doubt you, though appearances were against you when I returned to this house. All your chastity—enthusiasm—energy, love and faith—all were poured into this bosom. Can these things be forgotten? No, no, never! I am sure that when a man like you loves a woman like me, her memory never leaves him."

"You mistake!" he said dryly.

"And you, if you think that those fops at the marchioness' were not tricked and fooled by me! even the cheat who induced me to leave my home—you see, I am frank—he was my dupe, and I saw all the time his inferiority to the husband whom I quitted. In that case, it was a fortune that tempted me, for you know how pressed we were! But when alone, sobered—horrified by the warning conveyed in the sudden death of that man, I valued you correctly, and saw that I loved you above all men. I was subjected to the power of goodness and loving which is enthroned in you. All of a sudden, as you fell in love, I adored you, and if only you could have been kept in ignorance of what I did, there would have been no wife more faithful, devoted, submissive and loving than your own Césarine."

"Did I not forgive you when I learned of your faults?" he reproached her.

"True, you pardoned me," she answered, "but loftily, as one at a distance, shaking me off and regaining possession of yourself. In short, ceasing to be a man. You led me to see that you would no longer believe me, because I had once told a lie. Your behavior was grand, noble and lofty, for any other man would have whipped me out of his house like a cur; and yet I ought not to have been treated so."

"How? like a daughter of the Vieradlers—though you are probably not one?"

"You should have abused me, trampled me under foot, even—but then forgiven me like an erring man. I am earthly—worldly—and I do not understand grand sentiments and half-forgiveness."

There was some sense in her argument, but arguments would not have any effect on a character like his, which losing esteem once, was not to be deceived again. He had not required Hedwig's revelation about the web of treachery spun around him to be invulnerable to the pleading one. Her murder of her infant had ruined her irredeemably. Over it he had shed tears, though it was more in her image than his and, she had offered no one!

"Are we women more angelic than you men," she exclaimed the more feverishly, as she felt she was not gaining ground and that over the crumbling edge of which she vaguely hoped to climb, he would not stretch a hand in help. "Are faults, errors and failures your privilege, as force is? Did I really care for any of those men? Do I even recall one of them? It was only in rage and spite against your coldness that I went over to the marchioness. I ran to these flirtations to forget, as I would have taken morphine to sleep. But I have not forgotten you, and I have not slept off my love for you, and this is the truth!"

He made an impatient gesture.

"In short, nobody could wile away my heart. All those men together would not equal such a one as you, whom I loved and longed for. I do not wish to live—I was really ill in Paris, though you will not believe a word of it, and will not trouble to learn that I speak the truth—so ill that I sat at death's door and the peeping in terrified me. In that black cavern there was no love-light, and I crave for love! Then I discovered that I could not live without you, and that I was right to forgive you so much, though you will not forgive me heartily a little. See how abject I am! You are the master, but do not abuse your power. If I have no soul—inspire me with one—animate the statue of white clay—or share with me your own. We are bound to each other by sacred ties, and the marriage law must have been made by those who forsaw that the noblest and most generous of men might be wedded to the most guilty of women, but that he would save her. Rescue me!" she cried, sinking upon her knees.

"I am ready; what do you want?" he said in moved voice so that at last she began to hope.

"Forget my faults and the wrong they have caused you. I want you to forgive me everything up to the present minute—proudly hurl the past into dead eternity and make all that ought not to have been like what never was. Lastly, I crave for our departure for a change of sun and air and sky, so that the woman I mean to become henceforward should never be reminded for a single instant of the wretch that I was. Oh, let us live no more but for each other—you entirely mine as I entirely your own!"

Almost carried away by the eloquent outburst, Clemenceau had but one thought to cling to and hold him in the flood. His work of patriotism!

"Your work? well, there should be no work where love presides! after all," she continued, rising and venturing to slide her arms upon his shoulders, "you only toiled because you believed I did not love you. You tried to become celebrated only because you were not happy. You were a student when I opened the book of love to you and the little I showed you to read gave you the yearning for more. Labor came after love. When I caused you pain, you looked for consolation and you owe your genius to me. Genius understands or divines everything, and knows what human weakness is. Ah, if you had been weak and I mighty, how gladly I would have pardoned you! Had you done any wrong—if you were wrung by remorse like most of us—what joy to make you forget it. But no, you are honor itself, and I lose all hope?"

"Poor creature!" sighed he, but still like marble though her arms enfolded him and palpitate warm unlike serpents whose coils their curves resembled.

"You pity me?" she murmured coaxingly, although he did not thaw under her tightening clasp; "then, you agree?"

He shook his head. As usual, when perversity defends, the pleading reached the judge too late. Her pressure became irksome, he thought of the devilfish tightening its rings till fatal, and, by an effort, irresistible while gentle, he disengaged himself from her arms. They dropped inert by her panting sides as if broken. But only for an instant her defeat overpowered her.

"I see," she exclaimed, with a great change in her tone, "there is no more room in the heart which I deserted! You have replaced me with that Rebecca!"

"It is true I love her," her rejoined, "but not as you suppose. Do not try to understand how, for you cannot understand. Heaven knows that I would have wished to associate you with me in the same love and the same glory, but it is impossible. Once we were ships in company, sailing side by side—I thought with the same sailing orders—but you stole away in the night and I have had to direct my course alone toward a sea eternally forbidden to you. Oh, if you only knew how far I am already from you! The being who speaks to me by your lips is not known to me—I see her not! I do not know who you are. The only bond between us is the chain the law imposes—let us carry it between us but each with the share apart."

"What is to become of me?" cried Césarine, forced to try her last weapon. "You picked up a starving boy on the road and was kind to him. I am an outcast at your feet, hungry for love—succor me, no less kindly! I am a living creature, and I may be taught many things. Utilize me by your intelligence. Can I not be your pupil, your helper, your assistant? Do for me what Daniels has done for his daughter—initiate me into science, explain your labels to me and, associate me in your work."

"Teach you what you would sell!" he burst forth at the end of his endurance.

"Can you believe that?" she faltered, receding a step, turning white and trembling in the fear that he knew all.

"Believe? I am certain that you are lying now as always!" he thundered. "It is impossible that your remorse should be sincere; it must mask some infamy. You have perpetrated faults which are unattended by remorse. Enough! If I am wrong, and you really do repent, it will not take a minute, but years for you to be believed, and it does not concern me. Apply to the Church, which alone can redeem and absolve such culprits as you."

Convinced that she had lost the battle and forgetting her cunning, Madame Clemenceau threw off the veil and showed herself the direct offspring of the infernal regions. Her voice sounded like the hiss of fiery serpents, and her frame quivered as if she stood in a current of consuming vapor. Her eyes, too, wore that painful expression of depth of agony as though her disappointment were excruciating. With his pardon, love, protection and fortune, she might have defied Von Sendlingen and his league, but, alone, she was a stormy petrel flapping its insignificant pinions in the face of the God of Storms. Felix refused to be cheated by her and she was lost. But the criminal hates to stand alone in the dock; she wished to be terribly avenged because he was so great and so implacable. She would show that she could be extreme, too; if she were not encouraged to love, she would hate.

"Oh, you pitiless one, because you have right on your side and your conscience," she screamed; "I will drag you down with me into curses and blasphemies, and others as well! whoever you hold dear shall perish with us!"

"My father was threatened in the same way," retorted Clemenceau. "He had not the patience I enjoy. Had he but waited a little, the viper would have died in her own venomous slime!"

"Then you will not kill me as your murderer did my aunt?"

"No! you have wrecked my happiness, my home, my private life, but I forgive you, and that is your punishment. You have cast your wicked, unholy lures about my adopted son, Antonino, but I overlook this because he will repulse you and, that will be an augmentation of your punishment. You threaten Rebecca Daniels, but such are protected by the great Giver of good and, that is again an augmentation of your punishment. No, I will not hurt you—I would not kill one to whom long life—as it was to your witch grandmother, embitters every fraction of time. Live! and, remember, if you are here when I return, that our paths diverge forever here and beyond the earth!"

She had sunk in a heap on the tiger-skin rug and her hair, loosened by accident or perhaps by design, streamed in a sheet of graven gold over her faultless shoulders. Through this shimmering net, her tears flowed, detached like strung diamonds scattered from the thread. But her weeping and her attitude were thrown away, for she heard his step as regular as a soldier's, leaving the room, crossing the vestibule and taking him out to where the carriage wheels ground the gravel. Von Sendlingen had gone; the Daniels were descending the stairs; even the servants gave no sign of life. Already the doomed house began to sound with those dull echoes when spectres promenade where human tenants have dwelt. Under ordinary conditions, her place was to speed the parting guests, but her farewell to Rebecca had expressed her sentiments, and she dared not risk another contest of wits with the Hebrew.

She heard the horse's hoofs and the wheels beat the sand, and the click of the gate closing after the vehicle. The silence of death fell on the deserted house.

"I am alone," she said, sitting up but not rising.

"Now it will be everyone for himself and myself upon the side of evil, where they forced me to rank."

Hardly had she risen to her feet, very tremulous, and prepared to go to the mirror over the sideboard to re-arrange her hair, than she heard footsteps in the hall.

"Hedwig!" but listening more coolly, "no, a man!" she added, "has Von Sendlingen the audacity to enter?"

A man opened the door, but stood petrified on the threshold.

XXII

Felix

It was Antonino.

"Is this the keeper?" thought Césarine, laughing scornfully within herself. "A pretty boy for the austere Clemenceau to trust! Do not excuse yourself," she called out. "Close the door—it causes a draft! So, you told my husband that you loved me?"

Far from expecting this address, the Italian let several seconds pass before he faltered:

"Who told you so?"

"He did! he never lacks frankness, I will say that for him. Well, you have destroyed my chances of securing a peaceful life. And yet I never did you any harm, did I?"

"I destroy you?" repeated he, as she began to weep after a vain attempt to hide her eyes in her tresses.

"How is that?"

"Because I lost control of myself under his anger and his threats, and I confessed to him also that I was fond of you. We have a fellow feeling and selected the same confidant!"

"You love me?"

"For what else did I come back to this gloomy house? What else would have induced me to stay? He drove me away before, and I never suspected that it was to clear the scene for Rebecca, fool—child that I was! And now he picked the quarrel with me about you in order to go off with the heathen! You men are so monopolizing! He wants to be let love the inky-eyed Jewess, but I must not say a kind word to you! Oh, what am I to do now?" and in pretending to repair the disarray of her hair, down came a luxuriant tress. "What does it matter which way I turn? All roads lead to the river or the railroad—a step into the cold water or repose on the track of the iron horse, and no one will then torment poor Césarine!"

"You have some sinister plan," said Antonino, frightened by her manner. "I will not let you go away alone."

"Is it thus you guard your master's house?"

"Then wait till he returns and decide upon something."

"He will decide on separating us, that is sure. Do you think if he takes me, that you could go with us?"

"No! but if you meant to kill yourself, I should die after you."

"Why not die together?"

"I do not care."

"Then you love me thoroughly?" she exclaimed in delight.

"Death would be repose, and this struggle is driving me frantic," said he, in a deep voice.

"Well, we will die some day," she said with pretended fervor, "but we are young and have time before us. Lovers do not willingly die! If you love me as I love you, you would, like me, find life all of a sudden wondrously bright! What a blessing that I have money for our enjoyment!" clapping her hands like a child.

"In your fair Italy, we—"

"Money," repeated he, raised by her magic into a region above such sordid ideas and falling quickly.

"Of course! my bank orders! stay, they are in your box. Let us hasten away before he returns. Quick, take!"

"No;" said Antonino. "When he left the house in my charge he bade me touch nothing, and let nothing be touched until his return."

"He forsaw!" muttered the faithless wife, gnawing one of the tresses furiously as she studied the Italian's emotion. "Get me my money!"

"Wait until—"

"And with it those papers that describe your discoveries."

"What do you mean?" he cried, coming to a halt, half-way toward the chest while she was undoing one of the windows of which she had drawn back the curtains. "The papers—they are not mine, or yours."

"They will make the man I love rich and famous!" she replied, with eyes that seemed to light up the room far more than the starlight entering. "You know all about the work. With those plans in the language you also read, you can rise higher than he! He restricts his genius to his country—you—we will sell to the highest bidder!"

"Mercenary fiend! I comprehend all now!" said the Italian.

"So much the better!" she replied, coolly, having opened the window and descried a shadow standing guard in a narrow alley. "We shall lose no time in explaining."

"You mean to betray your country?"

"Neither mine nor yours! our country is wherever love and gold are rulers."

"Wretch!" cried he, taking a step toward her so threateningly that she retreated from the window to which his back was turned as he continued to face her.

"Which is the meaner?" she responded. "I deceive a man who loaths me, scorns me and threatens me with the love of another! You deceive the man who shelters you and to whom you owe everything. I betray him who does me harm—you, him who did you good. We are on a level, unless you have surpassed me. This is love! Did you imagine that you can withdraw the foot that takes one step in this path? An error, for one must tread it to the end. The steps are passion, the fault, the vice and the crime. But I have need of you to save me. I am yours and your soul is mine! Take the spoil and follow me!"

In his surprise, Antonino did not remark a footstep, sounding harsh with gravel grinding the wood of the verandah, or a grim face at the open window.

"You are right," he said. "I am a scoundrel, but I am not going to be a villain. It is I who should commit suicide. Farewell! my death be on your head!"

"You have spoken your doom!" said she quickly, as she made a sign to Von Sendlingen in whose hand she saw naked steel abruptly gleam.

"Who's there?" began the Italian, but, before he could turn, the long stiletto, drawn out of a sword-cane, was passed through his slender body.

He fell without a groan and his staring eyes, sublimely unconscious of his assassin and of the instigator of the crime, were riveted, on the ceiling.

"Confound it!" said the colonel, "this is not your husband!"

"No, another conscientious fool!" she said brutally. "Waste no time on that boy. Before the man returns, let us seize our prise. Keep your hands off. This is no common chest. It opens with a combination lock and the word is 'R-e-b-e-c-c-a!'"

She quickly fingered the studs which opened the lock when properly played upon, and to the joy of Colonel Von Sendlingen, she could lift up the loosened lid. But for a temporary vexation, they saw in the dim light that a kind of steel grating still closed the discovered space.

"That will not detain me long," said the colonel, contemptuously, and relying upon his great strength as he forced his fingers between these bars, he secured a firm hold and began to draw the frame up toward him. "You have done your part, madame, well, and I—"

At the same instant, the chest became a mass of the whitest flame which expanded monstrously and the whole house shook in a dreadful explosion.

It was supernaturally that Clemenceau had been warned to stand aside and let the justice of heaven deal its stroke. No longer fear that Césarine will work evil alone or directed by Von Sendlingen. At the last moment, all was put in order again by the execution by the soulless mechanism of the burglar defying-safe. The law of heaven shone forth in triumph and what was repentant in the errant soul was recalled to where goodness is omnipotent.

The flame leaped over the three dead bodies and seized upon the furniture, spreading in all sides. The timbers of the villa were old and kiln-dried. The proprietor, returning from the station, had a dreadful beacon to guide him.

All Montmorency turned out of doors to assist in extinguishing the conflagration. Not often does the quiet suburb treat itself to such spectacles, and when, to that sensation, was added that of three dead bodies dragged from the shattered drawing-room where every thing else was consumed, it may be believed that the night was memorable.

The Daniels were telegraphed to at Paris, and they returned before midnight. They alone knew that the grief of Clemenceau was given to Antonino and not to his wife, but the lookers-on were deceived, and many a man, returning to his slippers and the evening journal, scolded his wife for having repeated baseless scandals about the proprietor of the Reine-Claude Villa living on cool terms with his unfortunate wife.

The coroner of Montmorency did not display any broad perception of the tragedy, although the superfluity of eight inches of Sendlingen's steel in the side of a young man pronounced dead by asphyxia would have struck one of the laity. But the reporters of the Paris press were more perspicacious. They related that an envoy of a foreign union of unscrupulous capitalists had attempted to rob M. Clemenceau's residence of his inventions and France of a glory, but had been met by his dauntless wife and an assistant who had punished the brigand, although losing their own lives in defence of the patriotic trust. It was formed convenient to suppress all mention of the fact of the lady being Russian and the man Italian.

But in his death, Von Sendlingen gained some revenge. The loss of Antonino the detailed plans delayed Clemenceau in his project. The War farther threw them back and it was only recently that his perfected cannon was formally accepted. In all his tribulations and disappointments, Daniels supported him, for he, too, was an idealist, and so truly his friend as to defer his own scheme until he should be at ease.

After the fortuitous meeting of those men had come irresistible attraction and communion, moral, intellectual and scientific— friendship to the full meaning of the word.

Poetic justice, as we call the fate least like what man deals out, decreed that the château of the Marchioness de Latour-lagneau should be dilapidated during the Prussian occupation of Montmorency. On its ruins rises the manufactury of he new rifle. On the side of the heart, too, the same justice rewarded Clemenceau, for he married Rebecca, and they were happy in having sons to bear his name worthily. Césarine was forgotten, since, however great a conflagration may be—however far the flare may be cast on the sky—whatever the extent of damage—it must die out in time. Such is Passion, and the brighter its blaze the blacker the ruins it leaves after it—the deeper the misery—the wider the loneliness. It devours itself, with no revival like the Phoenix; but Love occupies the whole of life, however extended, and still has the strength and volumn to transport its worshipers to the realm of the happy.

A Note About the Author

Alexandre Dumas, fils (1824–1895) was a French writer and son of the famous novelist of the same name. He was born in Paris and formally educated at the Institution Goubaux and the Collège Bourbon. His earliest novel, *Aventures de quatre femmes et d'un perroquet* was published in 1847, followed by *Césarine* and his most notable work, *La Dame aux Camélias* in 1848. Despite his father's towering legacy, the young Dumas made a name for himself as an award-winning author and playwright.

A Note from the Publisher

Spanning many genres, from non-fiction essays to literature classics to children's books and lyric poetry, Mint Edition books showcase the master works of our time in a modern new package. The text is freshly typeset, is clean and easy to read, and features a new note about the author in each volume. Many books also include exclusive new introductory material. Every book boasts a striking new cover, which makes it as appropriate for collecting as it is for gift giving. Mint Edition books are only printed when a reader orders them, so natural resources are not wasted. We're proud that our books are never manufactured in excess and exist only in the exact quantity they need to be read and enjoyed.

Discover more of your favorite classics with Bookfinity™.

- Track your reading with custom book lists.
- Get great book recommendations for your personalized Reader Type.
- Add reviews for your favorite books.
- AND MUCH MORE!

Visit **bookfinity.com** and take the fun Reader Type quiz to get started.

Enjoy our classic and modern companion pairings!

Classic &
Modern

Bookfinity is a registered trademark of Ingram Book Group LLC. © 2023 Bookfinity. All rights reserved.

Printed in the USA
CPSIA information can be obtained
at www.ICGtesting.com
JSHW082148140824
68134JS00002B/35